TWISTED BEAUTY

TWISTED INTENTION
BOOK ONE

SUMMER COOPER

LOVY BOOKS

"It was written I should be loyal to the nightmare of my choice."

Joseph Conrad, Heart of Darkness

* * *

Keily

"Keily?" Violet's soft voice intruded into her thoughts and Keily looked over from her seat on her sister's spotless white couch to look at the three years younger, and three inches shorter, version of herself.

Keily was distracted, staring out of the window behind the couch, daydreaming of what should have been, instead of what was. "What?"

Her voice was disinterested, even a little rude. Her sister was always on her case about something and it had started to get old.

"I need you to watch Alice, please. I've got a late shift and the sitter can't come over." Her sister's voice came out more as a demand than a request but Keily wasn't in the mood. She'd had nightmares all night and the terror and fear she'd felt in the dream had bled into the daytime. She knew it was stupid to let something like that make her grumpy, but she couldn't help it. Anybody would be grumpy if they spent the entire night running from a shadowy man bent on murdering them.

It was best to distract herself, not let anything through that wall she'd built around herself years ago. Being soft wasn't how you got ahead in life, after all. You had to take no prisoners and act fast to stay ahead of the game.

"Alice through the looking glass?" She teased her sister over the choice of her daughter's name, for the millionth time.

It was a novel, or a movie, one of the two but Keily's amusement never ended over the phrase, even if her sister hated it. Teasing Violet was one of her favorite pastimes.

"Stop calling her that, and pick up after yourself, why don't you? Alice is barely a year old and she makes less of a mess than you do." Violet picked up an empty bag of chips and a can of iced tea that Keily hadn't bothered to throw away when she'd finished them two hours ago.

"You know, if Joe hadn't blown out his knee..." Keily started, stung by her sister's disapproval. She was on the defensive immediately, ready to attack.

"Yeah, yeah, if Joe hadn't blown his knee out in his last year at the university you'd be living in a mansion, with maids and a small army of servants to cater to your every whim. Well, the truth is, *big sister.*" Violet sneered that last part, "Joe did blow his knee and you didn't bother to get a degree. You were happy to ride on his dime, but now you're divorced, and you live with me."

"Well, at least I'm not a single mother with nobody to watch her kid." Keily sneered, her anger blasting past zero straight to a level of snark that couldn't be counted. "I didn't get pregnant with a guy that moved ten states away the minute he found out I was about to have his baby. You're just jealous of me, that's all."

Keily looked away, as if that was the end of the conversation. People had always been jealous of her, throughout her 25 years of life. In fact, she was fairly certain that the first memory she had was of her mother reassuring her that people were just jealous of her and that's why the other kids at the kiddy beauty pageants didn't like her.

"No, you just didn't get pregnant at all did you? I'm *so* jealous." Violet said, deadly quiet, her eyes full of tears that might have been regret at her own cruelty or hurt at the truth of what Keily had said. Violet blinked the tears away. "You divorced him, and now you live here, in abject poverty, with your *single mother* sister, living on *my* charity. If you'd stop feeling sorry for yourself and get a fucking job maybe you wouldn't hate everyone and everything so much, Keily. Earn a living for a change instead of expecting to be the prom queen forever, why don't you? Do you think you could do that, Keily?"

"Get somebody else to watch your brat for you, Violet. I have shit to do." Keily stormed up from the couch and moved to the door. She grabbed her handbag and left the two-bedroom apartment behind. She wasn't quite willing to admit that Violet had hit a very sore spot and struck a painful blow.

Fucking bitch, she thought to herself. Violet didn't understand, didn't know what it was like to be *her*, Keily Matthews Miller. This wasn't supposed to be her life, she knew that as her feet pounded along the sidewalk, the hard soles of her sandals a harsh sound on the concrete. She was supposed to be sitting with other football wives over cocktails around some bar in Cancun staring at pool boys and hot tourists while their husbands earned themselves concussions and multi-million-dollar paydays.

As the sun gleamed off her shoulders, bare to the sunlight in the pale blue sundress she wore, her tensions eased a little and she let her cares slip away. Her long blonde hair was tied up in a messy bun so even her neck got some of the sun's attention. Relief from the heat that bounced off the concrete in nearly visible waves was in sight, just a short little walk and she'd have some peace at last.

Keily didn't pay much attention to the direction her feet took; she knew where she was headed. There was a little bar at the end of the street, where she could usually talk some lonely businessman, or even a good ole boy, into buying her a few drinks for the price of a smile and a little flirtation. It was almost three pm, but she didn't care, it wasn't like she had anything better to do.

Violet would find a sitter, she always did, and Keily was a free woman, she could do whatever she wanted. She'd pretended for months now that she was looking for a job, but she hadn't actually even opened a paper, much less written up a resume. She'd made Joe sell the house they'd bought together, but most of that money had gone to pay off the mortgage they owed on it.

For a while, she'd had a little bit of money, but that dried up two months ago, and now, a year after her divorce, she had exactly $4.86 left in her checking account and $2.77 in her pocket. She walked into the bar and went right up to the bartender. She wiped away the sweat from the July heat outside with a couple of napkins she pulled off the bar.

"My usual, Henry." She told the older man behind the bar. His face was deeply wrinkled but his hair was still black. The wrinkles and his gray beard gave away his age. She wondered if he dyed his hair that color and narrowed her eyes as he stared back at her with derision.

"You got money today or are you going to fleece my customers again?" The man asked, but he poured vodka into a glass of ice and orange juice as he spoke.

"Now, when have I ever had to pay for a drink, Henry?" She gave him a flirty wink despite his sneer and took the drink from him. With the straw pressed between her lips, Keily sipped the drink and sighed through her nose. "I needed that."

"Tough day at work, huh?" Henry asked, no sarcasm detectable, but Keily's eyes narrowed anyway.

"Something like that." She'd never told him anything about her work circumstances or her home life, how would he know if she had a job or not?

The way he sneered at her reminded her of the argument she'd had with her younger sister. Violet had come along when Keily was three, a force to be reckoned with on the best of days. She always seemed to doubt Keily, even when they were children.

Don't be so sensitive, her mother used to tell her, and she heard that advice now. There weren't enough men in the place right now, but there would be soon enough.

She ignored the regulars, the ones she'd already blown off, and waited for a new one to come in. Henry's place was right off the interstate and lots of lonely guys came in looking for a place to have a quick drink, maybe find a lady to spend the night with.

Keily never went home with any of them, but she'd gladly spend an evening telling them about her past exploits. About how she'd been homecoming queen, prom queen, queen of all of the pageants, she'd even been Miss Teen South Carolina her senior year of high school. She'd been queen of it all in her younger years. She'd had the best boyfriend in the whole of King's Hill, South Carolina too. All the girls hated her because Joe only had eyes for her.

But, as Violet had so rudely pointed out, Joe had injured his knee right before he signed a contract with one of the biggest teams in the NFL. It was the second to last game of his senior year at the University of South Carolina and he was going to sign the contract the next day. That hadn't happened. A tackle took him down but more importantly, it took down his NFL career before it even started.

Keily hadn't even applied to a university to get a degree because she'd planned to be Joe's wife from day one. He'd make the money, she'd make babies, direct housekeepers, and sip coffee with her new BFFs around her pool. That had been the plan anyway.

They'd married right before he went off to USC and lived in a house his dad had paid for. His dad also provided them with expense money, up until Joe finished his degree in communications. Then he cut them off.

Keily had tried to be supportive, she'd done her best to learn to cook meals, instead of them indulging their nightly habit of dining out, she'd tried to learn to clean the house, and do without getting her nails done. Or her hair.

Joe had never recovered from the emotional blow.

He'd started to drink, and then he stopped eating. She'd put up with him for years, done the drunken brawls together, done the silent days of hangovers, until the final humiliation had driven her away. Keily pushed that memory away and looked across the bar, her glass almost empty.

She spotted a 40-something looking guy dressed like a banker in the corner off by himself and sashayed over to him. "Care to buy a lady a drink?"

Keily used her most husky, sensual voice as she trailed her fingers along the table and looked up at him from mascara-darkened eyelashes. She had to use the cheap crap Violet bought, but it did the trick.

"Sure, have a seat." The portly man pointed at the empty chair with a surprised smile and she sat down. "I don't have long, but I could use some company. What'll it be?"

The man went to order her drink and came back. She learned he was married, not looking for anything else, but he didn't mind talking to her while he waited for a meeting he had to get to up on Main Street. The man soon left, but he bought her another drink before he left so Keily was happy to see him go.

She took out her phone and noticed her carrier had finally turned her phone off. "Henry, what's the Wi-Fi password?"

Henry pointed at a sign on the wall. "Use your own Wi-Fi, we aren't giving it away"

Her middle finger itched to stick up at him, but she turned away.

"Here, read the paper instead." Henry walked up to the table and plopped down the local paper.

With a quick arch of an eyebrow, she noticed it was open to the classifieds. Help wanted. "Really, Henry?"

"Really, Keily. Get a job."

Her lungs inflated as she sucked in air to spew out an angry retort, but she squashed it. This was the only bar within walking distance and she didn't have a car. It was best not to piss Henry off.

Instead, she huffed and pulled a pen out of her purse to pretend to examine the want ads. She doodled obscene pictures on the paper until something caught her eye. There was a new tech company in town and they wanted people with skills. One of the positions listed was personal assistant. The benefits listed caught her eye.

Company car, great salary, company phone and laptop, vacation days, healthcare package, and other benefits. Hmm. She'd been Joe's personal slave for years, surely she could wait on a sober CEO for all of that. She'd have to fiddle her resume a little, heck, she'd have to make one first, but then she was certain she could get the job. With a baleful glare at Henry, she tore out the section of the paper and put it in her bag.

She'd go home and use Violet's computer to find out how to make a resume and try to see if she could find enough change to take the bus into town. She'd raid Alice's piggy bank for a couple of dollars if she had to. Violet wouldn't notice.

With one last glare at Henry, Keily got up and left the bar, a little less steady than when she'd walked in. Her walk back to Violet's place was uneventful and she soon walked in the door to find Jenny, a teenager from across the street, watching a movie with Alice who was asleep on the couch.

For a moment, regret tightened her chest. She should be watching Alice. Violet worked really hard and was devoted to the girl and, truthfully, Keily loved Alice as much as any aunt should. She just couldn't afford to spoil her and right now, the world was still upside down as far as Keily was concerned. She still had no idea which direction to go in or who to follow and her words earlier were a result of that directionless feeling. She'd have to find a way to apologize to her sister, without actually admitting she was at fault.

"Oh, hey Keily," Jenny said and put a gentle hand on Alice's back. *As if to protect the baby from me*, Keily thought with a troubled expression. Her hackles went right back up and irritation thrummed through, to erase that moment of regret.

It was more than obvious that Alice was related to her Aunt Keily. The family all had the same intriguing light gray eyes, the same heart-shaped faces, and the same ash-blonde hair. They were all beautiful, but something about Keily was different. There was a meanness in her face that she couldn't hide, that Violet and Alice lacked. Keily stared at the baby that could be hers, if she hadn't been on birth control the entire time she was with Joe, at his insistence. Guilt gnawed at Keily for calling the baby a brat, but she squashed that as she did most things that bothered her.

"Hi, Jenny, she suckered you again, huh?" Keily drawled and slipped her sandals off.

"It's no problem, really. I can use the cash anyway." Jenny said without a hint of spite.

Keily heard the accusation though. *Why am I here,*

Keily, shouldn't you watch your sister's kid for free since you haven't even paid her rent for two months?

Or was that her conscience eating at her, she wondered.

The computer was in the kitchen so Keily walked in there without another word to the teenager on the pristine white couch. Keily had a feeling that white couch wouldn't stay so pretty once Alice got a little older, and some spiteful part of her couldn't wait for that day.

The two-bedroom apartment was laid out like a giant square box. Two bedrooms in the back, a bathroom on the left side with the kitchen on the same side. Each room was its own little box, except for the living room which was open without any doors or walls. It made the apartment feel bigger, even though it was small.

Keily walked into the kitchen to see her sister had thrown away her empty can and chip bag, but she'd left the full bag of trash in the can. Keily assumed that meant she should take it out, but she had things to do. She sat down at the small desk where Violet had set the computer up in a corner of the kitchen and set to work.

She found the company online, saw that there was a section to apply for a job online, and started to fill in the questionnaire that was part of the process. She chose every word carefully and made certain that her answers were full of confidence and the kind of thing employers would want to hear. She was stumped when it came to the resume part though. She didn't have one because she'd never had a job before.

Her next search was 'how to write a resume'. Then she looked up examples and started to type from a template she found online. Almost every word was a lie, she'd never been to USC as anything other than a supporter at the football games or to drop Joe off at classes. She didn't have a degree in anything, much less English literature. All she had was a high school diploma, but how likely was it anyone would check for such a low-level position as a personal assistant? She listed a fake company and her experience with Joe as her credentials.

Reason for leaving?

Hmm, now that one stumped her for a bit until inspiration hit again. "Owner died and company closed."

That way she didn't have to prove she'd ever worked for them. Or hadn't.

She added in a few fake employment awards and a fake GPA for everything. She printed the resume to have a copy of it on hand. She wouldn't want to forget what she'd said in all that, now would she? She copied a cover letter and filled in the blanks, but she couldn't figure out how to delete the underlining out of the text. She printed it anyway, hit send once she'd uploaded the files, and then went to take a shower. She'd find a few dollars for the bus fare and head downtown early tomorrow morning.

Then she'd not only look punctual, but her beauty would swamp any competition. With a smile of pure confidence, Keily connected her phone to Violet's Wi-Fi and found a movie on her sister's Netflix account to watch. That kept her busy until she fell asleep, perfectly sure she'd get the job because she was Keily Matthews Miller. She was someone special, someone that mattered, someone that deserved a good life because she just did. It never occurred to her to wonder why she was so damn special. Her mother had always said she was, so she was. That was the end of it.

2

Logan

"Logan, how are you, boss?" The voice came over the sound system of his new black Cadillac CT6-V.

Logan loved that feature, loved the car, and tightened his fingers on the steering wheel in appreciation of how smoothly the car responded to his slightest touch.

"I'm good, Wally, how are you?" Logan watched the traffic around him as he headed to the new house he'd bought, along with the car. He was going to be in town for a while, for a long while, so he'd decided he'd take some of those piles of cash he'd earned since he'd graduated from Florida State University and buy himself a few luxuries. The car was one of those luxuries.

He'd got off the private jet that brought him back to

King's Hill, South Carolina, and took possession of the keys to the car right away. All mine, he'd thought as he walked around the car, admiring the lines and curves of the beast he'd ordered and had delivered to the airport. When he got in and figured out how to sync his phone up with the sound system, he'd called Wally, his second in command at his company over in California.

"I'm great, Logan, what can I do for you?" Wally asked.

"I just wondered how everything is going out there?" Logan steered the car towards the turn his navigation system quietly indicated he should make while he was on the call and continued. "I know I've only been gone a couple of days, but I wanted to check-in."

"Everything is fine at Sinclair Personal Security Industries, Logan, I promise. The company is safe with me." Wally's confident voice eased Logan's worries, and he smiled, his brown eyes gleaming brightly as the head-lights of another car bounced across his face.

"That's good, Wally, because I'll have your balls if you fuck my company up," Logan responded, only half-joking. Wally knew it too.

"Of course, and I wouldn't blame you. All is well here though and I'm about to send the daily reports from each department to your email." Wally's smooth voice filled the confines of the car, and Logan nodded, his dark brown hair, a little too long on top, but still stylish, moved with his nod.

"Glad to hear it. I'm about to pull into my driveway, once I get settled in, I'll have a look at the reports." Logan turned onto the white gravel road and then stopped in front of the isolated house he'd only seen in video or pictures so far. He'd bought it after a thorough inspection, and with the location in mind.

The house wasn't located in a suburb, but it was one of the richest areas of King's Hill. This house had been in his sights since he was a teenager and it was first built. The exterior was an odd mixture of granite and wood, with a black roof. Shaped like an "L' turned on its back, the left side of the house resembled a log cabin, while the right side was two stories of marble exterior mixed with more logs.

The richest man in King's Hill had the house built but he'd died, and the man's kid didn't want the house. Logan had snapped it up, fulfilling a dream he'd had since the house was first constructed. He was now the man with the most money in this town and he wanted everyone to know it. He could have wasted time and had a bigger, better house built, but he didn't want to wait around, so he'd bought this place. The keys were in the glove box, and he took them out before he got out and took his bags from the backseat.

The furniture and appliances had already been delivered and set up, while a newly hired maid had ensured the fridge was full of the items he'd asked for and made sure the place was ready for his arrival. He smiled as he opened the front door on the left side of the house and smelled the homey scent of baked apple pie. The maid had found his favorite candle and lit it.

It was a quirk of his, the fact that he loved that scented candle so much, but he didn't really think about it or question it. He liked the scent, so he kept buying the candles. Logan closed the door and walked further into the house. The door opened into a spacious living room with a tall ceiling. The black leather couch and recliner rested on a hardwood floor, with a glass and gold-colored metal coffee table between the two. A smart TV hung on the wall, large enough to fill a good proportion of it. A window to the right of the TV might make viewing difficult when the sun was out, but he would rarely be home before the sun went down, even on the weekend.

He didn't get to billionaire status by demanding weekends off or shirking his duties. He'd worked hard to build his company up from a small business that sold goods online to the manufacturer and seller of security essentials people could buy in stores and online. His company manufactured items like test kits for date-rape drugs in drinks, small tasers for personal defense, personal alarms that would emit a loud screeching noise, and many other items. Their newest product was a watch that would call the police at the press of a button and send the wearer's location to the police department.

The new factory would manufacture the bulk of those watches and any new products that Logan and his team designed. Tomorrow, experts would start installing the manufacturing equipment in the factory and he'd start hiring staff. He would personally hire the professional staff, the human resources director, supervisors, and office staff. He'd start with a PA, he decided.

That person would be essential in helping him as he began the process of opening a new business in his hometown. The fact that this place had been a nightmare for him in the past was part of the reason he was back. The people here had forgotten about him once he left and most wouldn't even know who he was. He'd grown into a man well over six feet tall, with broad shoulders and a muscular frame.

The weak, acne-covered kid had become a man to be reckoned with, and he was back to show them all they'd been wrong about him. He'd made something of himself, and now he'd get back at everyone that had made his life hell. He'd been a geeky kid, wanting nothing more than to escape the town, so it was a little strange to be back, to own the house he'd dreamed about owning, to know that he'd finally get his own back against everyone that had made him miserable. If they were still alive.

He knew one of the kids he'd graduated with had died in a car accident a week after their graduation. Others had ended up in jail, or they'd overdosed on one drug or another. Time hadn't been kind to King's Hill and as manufacturers moved their operations to China or Mexico, jobs had dried up and people began to lose hope. Not all of them had, though, and Logan would live it up knowing he was better off than all those that had hurt him, in one way or another.

His plans weren't all about payback, though. He knew people here needed jobs and that they would work hard to keep his company there, once they saw he was a fair employer who brought more to the community than it took out of it. That was his plan for the future, but tonight, he wanted a sandwich, a shower, and to get to bed.

He'd spent the last week finalizing plans for his move and now he was exhausted, glad he'd hired staff to unpack his boxes, hang his suits, and put his other clothes away, and to make the bed up for him. Some boxes he'd marked as personal and the maid had left those alone, as directed, but the rest of his items like kitchenware and bath towels had all been unpacked and put away.

After a quick ham sandwich and a hot shower, Logan

slipped into a pair of black sweatpants, and slid into bed. He set his alarm for 5 am, his normal wakeup time, and tried not to think about the past. He tried not to remember the football team or the variety of ways they'd found to torture him. He tried not to remember the humiliation and disgrace he'd been to his family when he'd been unable to fight back against the other, bigger boys.

They'd never come on their own, one at a time. Oh no, there'd always been at least three or four of the bastards, ready to punch his lights out, or hold him down and pull his pants off. They'd have a hard time doing that now, even if there were more than one of the fuckwits. Let them try.

Logan ran through the accomplishments he'd managed since he went off to FSU and became Logan Sinclair, instead of Eugene Baumgarten. His original birth certificate said that was his name, but the new certificate, the one with his middle name and his mother's maiden name bore the name he used now. His legal name now and the man he really was, not that young man he'd once been.

When he went to FSU and changed his name, he became the guy every girl wanted, but not every girl could have. He was picky about who he slept with and chose only the best, the girls with sad eyes that needed a man to show them they were alive, even if it was only for one night. He never chose the cheerleaders or the popular girls back then. Nope, he chose the ones that needed him as a lover, not a notch in their belts.

He was still that same picky man, but he'd give the other women a chance now and, still single, probably would for a long time. Most women wanted a man that came home before 9 at night, that could take time off work to go to the movies or out on dates. They wanted a man that could take them out to dance and drink, have fun, things Logan never had time to do.

He thought about one girl from the past, one in particular, who had nearly broken him completely. A girl that surpassed all the others and filled his memory as he drifted off to sleep. A woman he'd never have because even if she was still around, he wouldn't let her near his heart, ever again.

LOGAN ARRIVED at the office next to the factory at 6:30 am. After running five miles around the woods of his home, he'd worked out in his home gym, then showered, had breakfast, dressed in one of his many tailored suits, and went off to work. He'd noted the sprawling Olympic-sized swimming pool at the back of the house, but he didn't have time for a swim. Maybe when he got home later in the evening, but not this morning.

He walked into the office, glad to see the temporary agency had sent out the janitorial staff to set up his office and the other offices in the three-story glass building. He'd need a doorman, security staff at the entrance to the office, just in case, and clerks for a variety of departmental offices. The building was big enough to house all of those offices with his office on the top floor.

One of the benefits of the location was that it was near a bus stop and there were a few small restaurants and cafes on one side of the street to feed the workers from the factories that lined the other. A lot of the factories had closed down over the years, but there were still enough to keep the restaurants open. And now, he'd provide them with more hungry workers to feed.

He found the office set up for his personal use, put a pot of coffee on to brew, and checked the small fridge hidden behind the façade of a cabinet door. He put in the drinks, fresh milk for his coffee, and a few healthy snacks he'd bought at the large grocery store on his way to the office. With a sigh of contentment, he went to his desk, took his laptop out of his black messenger bag, and started to open emails.

He went through the reports Wally had sent, then saw that he already had applications on the website for positions at his South Carolina facility. He went through the ones marked as personal assistant applications first.

One name caught his eye, and the picture she'd somehow inserted into the resume certainly drew attention.

Keily Matthews Miller. She wasn't exactly what he was looking for, not really, but she was experienced, even if she only had one previous position that seemed to qualify her for the PA job. The other applicants were either not qualified or had done sloppy work filling out the questionnaire he'd designed purposely to weed out those not qualified for the position.

Her answers oozed confidence, ability, as well as arrogance and self-assuredness. For a moment, he wondered about her resume, about that one position. It was rather convenient that the owner of the place had died not long ago. He'd have to look the place up, see if it had actually existed, but then, he decided it didn't matter.

This was an opportunity, a chance to get started, and if it didn't work out, well, he'd just find someone to replace her, even if he had to bring someone out from California. He sent back an email to her, directing her to arrive at his office at one later that afternoon. Let's see if she'd actually show up - he had to wonder if she would. Someone that confident wouldn't enjoy being a PA, he thought.

Maybe she would, he decided as he looked her up online. Recently split from her husband, former cheerleader, just the kind of woman that he wanted to avoid. But Keily was offering herself up on a platter to him and she didn't have a criminal record. The problem was, he couldn't look away from her almost colorless gray eyes. He hadn't been able to resist girls like her in high school either, but he wasn't that same gullible kid. Now he was a full-grown man and he wouldn't be one that lived each new day as a fresh hell. Not anymore.

3

___

Keily

*K*eily woke up with a smile on her face. She wasn't sure why, but she had a feeling it was her lucky day. Even if Alice was screaming her head off already.

Keily got out of bed and picked up her phone, put in her earbuds, and put on some music to drown Alice out. Violet had come home late, but the baby was hers, not Keily's. Besides, she had email to check.

Another piercing wail made Keily sigh and she put down her phone to see to Alice. It wasn't like she didn't know how to care for the baby, it was just that, well, she didn't want to get too attached to her. Holding Alice brought out all of these *feelings* in Keily. Feelings she didn't like. Regret, longing, the need to have someone to love were almost too much to carry when she held Alice. But she needed to keep the baby quiet.

She went in and picked the baby up, shushed her, and wiped her face dry before she changed her diaper. Keily softly sang a lullaby as she went into the kitchen and fed the baby with one hand while she turned her phone on with the other.

Her fingers shook a little as she punched at the one email response that she hadn't dreamed would come so quickly. Was it a 'thanks for your interest, but we regret the position has been filled' email or a 'come and see us' email? Her finger missed the email she wanted to open and opened one from a clothes seller she'd clicked on by accident one time. She had a habit of not clicking on the right thing.

Violet said she needed glasses, but Keily knew better. Everything about her was perfect, from her body to her vision. There was no need to spend money on an eye exam when she knew good and well that her vision was fine. Even if she did have to squint at things that were small, like the letters on her phone screen when she held it too far away.

She closed the email promising to sell her a beautiful dress for pennies, which she knew would be second or third quality, not the first quality promised, and opened the one she wanted to read the most. Still in her pajamas, teeth unbrushed, hair wild around her head, Keily's mouth dropped open when she saw an invitation to interview later that afternoon. She'd planned to go check out his office this morning, but it seemed Logan Sinclair had other ideas.

Fine, that would just give her time to get ready at her leisure then. She pulled out her earbuds, dropped her phone, and got out of her room. Violet came into the kitchen just as she was preparing to take Alice out of her highchair and take her to her mother. Keily glanced up at Violet with a blank look, yesterday's argument still fresh in her mind.

"I've found a daycare that will keep her for me." Violet sighed as she picked up Alice and sat down in a chair.

"Good." Keily ignored her sister's accusatory tone.

It was none of her business what Violet did with Alice. The baby was none of her concern, even if Violet's tone suggested that a good aunt would have offered to watch the baby, especially when she was living with Keily for free.

Not her baby, not her problem.

"I have a job interview today, so it's not like I could watch her anyway," Keily said, voice slightly snippy.

"Really, Keily? An interview?" Violet turned to look at her sister, doubt etched on her lean face. Violet's weight had plummeted recently, Keily noted. She should do something about that anxiety, Keily thought but still, guilt ate at her, so she turned that guilt back to her sister as anger.

"You think I'm lying? Here, look." Keily picked her phone up and opened the email to show Violet. Violet's face changed from doubt to amazement as she looked at her sister.

"Well, then, good luck. I hope it works out for you." Violet's smile tugged only at the corners of her mouth and didn't spread all the way across as Keily hoped it would. She still doubted Keily's ability to get the job then. That was a real kick to her confidence, Keily realized, as she pulled the phone away.

"Thanks." The word came out mumbled, and she walked away, her normal confident demeanor now a million miles away.

Looking through her closet didn't help. She didn't want to admit it to anyone, but she'd had to sell a lot of her jewelry and clothes to keep herself going. All her pretty clothes, always new and fashionable, had slowly dwindled down to a small wardrobe that she could mix and match to make it look like she wasn't wearing the same outfit repeatedly. Her eyes moved along the rail, down to the very end, where she'd hidden away a navy-blue pantsuit, just in case something important came up.

With a pair of black pumps, the outfit would be suitable, even if the long sleeves of the jacket would make her uncomfortable. She could walk in wearing it but take it off after a few minutes. That would work, she decided, and pulled the suit out along with a white silk blouse she'd saved.

Keily heard a sound at her door and turned around. Violet stood there, Alice on her hip. "If you get this job, *if*, does that mean you'll start helping out with the bills?"

Why did she have to put so much emphasis on the word if, Keily thought with a frown. She might have told a few white lies, she might not actually be qualified to be a personal assistant, but she could win any man over, with just the right smile. She'd learned that a long time ago.

Keily lifted her chin in the air and looked back at her sister and niece with fire in her eyes. "Look, I know you're mad because you had to get daycare for Alice, but I know nothing about babies, it would be dangerous to leave her with me, wouldn't it?"

"What's that got to do with paying bills?" Violet asked softly, and Keily raised her chin a little higher.

If Violet wanted to be angry, she could give it back.

"Nothing, I suppose, but that doesn't make it untrue, does it?" Keily pushed past her sister and headed for the bathroom. Her sister would leave her alone there, at least.

"Why is she always on my case about the damn bills?" She muttered to herself as she locked the door and turned away. "It's not like she's poor or anything."

Keily got ready slowly, she had a lot of time to spare. A look at the bus schedule showed her that she'd either have to take the bus that came at noon or miss her appointment because the next bus didn't arrive until 1:15 pm. It meant sitting at the bus stop or sipping a coffee at a café somewhere.

Before her split with Joe, she'd had a car, and never wasted time waiting on a bus. She hated it, but there was nothing else she could do about it. With a sigh of frustration, Keily went into Alice's bedroom. Alice had a plastic piggy bank sitting on her dresser that was full of coins. Coins that Keily needed.

Keily stopped for a minute as guilt washed over her the moment her hands went near the piggy bank. Maybe it was better to look under the couch cushions first and see what loose change she might find. It wasn't right, taking money from her niece, and she knew it.

A quick glance at the clock on the wall showed her that she still had an hour to kill before she went to the bus stop. Ten minutes later she'd found $38 in an old handbag that she'd nearly thrown away but kept because it was a designer bag. Tears pricked at her eyes as she thought about the days when she could just shove money into her bags like that and forget about it. The days when she had everything she wanted. Well, nearly everything.

Joe's drinking problem had only grown as time went

on and life had started to get harder and harder. At least she had bus fare and money for a cup of coffee now, she thought as she swiped at the tears and stiffened her spine. And she hadn't had to rob her niece.

As she walked out of the home she shared with her sister and niece, jacket carefully folded over her arm, Keily's confidence came back and she held her head up proudly. Her hair was tucked up into a perfect French twist, and her makeup was applied expertly. She'd had to scrape the last drops of her primer out of the tube, but oh well. If she got this job, she could buy new makeup, new clothes, and eventually make it out of Violet's home.

She hated living with her sister, but it was the only real option she had. To go anywhere else would just be shameful. She couldn't handle that.

She was the only one there when she arrived at the bus stop. There wasn't much reason to look at her phone, there'd been no notifications, and she didn't care about the news, so she looked down the street, just staring off into space. It was something she'd learned to do when she first started dating Joe and all he cared about was football. Over time, his stories had become boring, and she'd heard them all, so as he regaled their friends and acquaintances with his past glories, she'd learned to disconnect from the world around her.

"Hello, dear, you look nice today."

Keily looked back to see old Mr. Henderson tottering up to the bus stop. He went out every day to get his food and to chat with people at the bus stop and on the bus. She suspected he was lonely, and this was a way to alleviate that. She'd charmed him weeks ago, simply by listening to him politely, and now when he saw her, he always spoke kindly to her.

He was ninety if he was a day, with no hair at all on his liver-spotted head, and his back was bent in a way that must be painful. But he kept upright with the help of a cane and sheer willpower.

"Hello, Mr. Henderson, how are you today?" Keily dipped her head at him and gave him a polite smile.

He settled onto the other end of the bench, put his hands over the top of each other on the cane he parked between his legs, and smiled. His dentures were spotless and pearly white.

"I'm doing alright, my dear. Doing alright." He took a deep breath and then nodded. "It's my birthday today, thought I'd go get myself a bite of cake."

"That sounds lovely." Keily knew it was impolite to ask him his age, her mother had taught her that a long time ago, so she just smiled and wished him a happy birthday.

"Thank you. Mighty kind of you." He grinned this time, his light blue eyes rheumy, but still somehow full of life.

"Not at all. I do hope it's a nice birthday, you're a nice man."

"Well, here's the bus. I hope you have a nice day, dear." Mr. Henderson struggled to stand up, but he managed it without assistance.

Keily didn't offer to help, but she did allow him to climb onto the bus first. He took the first seat available near the front, but she headed for the middle. The ride wasn't too long and before she knew it, she was having coffee. She filled the time watching people walk by from behind her sunglasses.

She'd chosen a café across from the building she needed to go to. It was in the more industrialized part of town, and she noted there was a factory directly next to it. She sat facing the building and hoped she'd see the owner of the place before she went in. Nobody went into the office building or the factory, and nobody came out, so she was disappointed.

At five minutes to one, she walked across the street and opened the door to the office. There was a reception area to the right, but there wasn't anyone sitting at the wide orange-colored desk that filled that side of the small area. There was a door behind the desk, but it was closed. There was a row of six orange plastic seats in front of the glass pane that served as a wall. Keily frowned in confusion, glanced at the elevator to the left, then at the chairs. She considered taking the elevator up to one of the floors but which one?

She decided to just sit in one of the chairs for now and wait. She crossed her legs at the ankle, arranged her jacket and handbag on another chair, and waited. Surely, someone would come down to get her?

Ten minutes later, Keily was fuming and ready to leave. This was just rude, leaving her down here like this. She'd stood up to leave when she heard the elevator ding. Her demeanor changed instantly from a frown of anger to schooled politeness. Her lips even tilted up a little at the corners to convey a polite smile.

"Keily?" A gorgeous man asked as he stepped off the elevator. He was tall, well-dressed in a dove-gray tailored suit that fit his frame perfectly, with a smile that must have cost his parents a fortune.

"That's me." She spoke almost breathlessly as she took the man in. Dark brown hair cut short around the back and sides but fashionably long on top, just enough to get her fingers into, she thought before she blinked at him. Where had that thought come from?

She'd only ever been with Joe, but one look at this man and all thought left her head. He was about her age and his grin was charming, self-assured, like so many she'd seen on more than her fair share of handsome men. There was something about this one though, something she couldn't put her finger on. Something that made her brain stutter with…attraction?

"I'm Logan Sinclair. Won't you follow me, please?" He held the elevator door open with one hand and shook hers with the other.

"Of course, Mr. Sinclair." She stared up into golden-brown eyes as he shook her hand, completely entranced with how big his hand was, how much those eyes peered into her soul.

When he smirked at her, she pulled her hand away. *What the fuck*, she thought, *I'm Keily Matthews Miller, men don't smirk at me, I smirk at them.* Her eyebrows knitted together as she stepped into the elevator, confusion rippling through her. Who did he think he was?

Tailored suit or not, she didn't give a damn. She stood behind him and ran her eyes over his back, which was a mistake because she could see the strength of the muscles beneath the fabric of his suit jacket. And, *damn, he has a nice ass.* She tried to look away, but couldn't, and her hands itched to palm the two perfectly round globes that begged to be touched. She inhaled swiftly, trying to distract herself but that only brought his scent to her nostrils, and she found herself leaning towards him, to inhale more of it. He smelled so damned good.

Who was this guy? She should have looked him up before she came here, why hadn't she thought to do that? Fuck, now she had no idea who he was, if he was married, though she hadn't seen a ring, or if he was some kind of criminal. For all she knew, now that it had finally occurred to her, he was luring women here to murder them and then hide their bodies in that huge warehouse next door.

He chose that moment to cast a glance back at her, just before the bell dinged and the elevator stopped. Was that lifted eyebrow a challenge?

"Ready?" His deep, rich voice, husky almost, made her skin prickle. His eyes most definitely challenged her to step off the elevator and into the unknown.

"Yes." She said with a tilt of her chin and a snippy tone in her voice. "Whenever you are."

She challenged back, not even thinking about the fact that she needed a job - now. Or whether or not he was some kind of mass murderer. She just wanted to wipe that smirk off his face.

"Good, I'm looking for someone that can face any...*challenge* I throw their way." His voice came from behind her, but she wasn't about to dignify that little allusion of his with a response.

Any challenge indeed, she thought, her left eyebrow high on her forehead as she walked ahead of him. We'll see about that.

4

Logan

"Please, this way." Logan turned on the charm as he walked ahead of the rather delectable and shapely Keily Matthews, now Miller.

He wondered why she hadn't dropped her ex-husband's last name, but didn't really care, he decided, as she walked into his office through the door he'd opened for her.

"Take a seat." He instructed as he sat down behind his desk and opened her file. He'd printed off everything she'd sent in, including the answers to his questionnaire. "Tell me about yourself, Ms. Miller."

"Oh, okay." She moved around in her seat, as if flustered. She put her suit jacket and handbag on the chair next to her and looked him right in the eye with a smile he knew was meant to charm his socks right off.

He guessed she'd expected some small talk, a little bit of an introduction to the company, but that wasn't how he wanted to do this. He needed someone that could think fast, give answers that made sense, and was capable of responding to a demanding job. The smile was disarming, but she wasn't dealing with the average guy. He was immune to charm, after all, he used it himself at every opportunity.

"I was born here in King's Hill, lived here most of my life, except for when I went off to get my degree, of course." Her eyes narrowed for a moment and he made note of it. A lie perhaps?

"So, you know the place well?" He asked, just to prompt her into going on.

"Like the back of my hand." She tilted her chin up, something he'd already noticed she did a lot.

Defiance, good.

"Great. So, tell me about your experience at your last job." He demanded almost immediately after she answered, and she blinked at him.

"My last job?" She asked blankly, and he knew then there was a lie or two in her resume, but then she started to recover. "I'm sorry, it was just such a sudden loss, you know, with the owner passing away, getting divorced, and well, losing my job too, it's been rough. But I can tell you that I was responsible for making all of Mr. Brown's appointments, taking his phone calls, keeping his schedule up to date, picking up his dry cleaning, arranging his business dinners as well as charitable galas he wanted organized, and made sure he wasn't bothered when he wanted peace and quiet. I also arranged for meals when he was at the office late, made sure his staff at home kept the place organized and neat, and a lot of other things that I imagine are similar to the things I'd do for you."

"I see." He turned on his own charm then and gave her the smile that had dropped more panties than a gynecologist's office. "Tell me, what are these…*other things* you imagine you'd do for me?"

"Oh, um." Her eyes went wide for a moment, but then the red that flooded her cheeks disappeared and she got ahold of herself. "I imagine I'd arrange cars for you when you traveled, travel plans of any kind, handle communications with the rest of your staff, and anything else you might need me to do."

Confidence oozed from every pore barely visible on her flawless face and Logan leaned in closer. "Right. Anything else?"

He lifted a dark eyebrow and leaned in closer. Her cheeks didn't turn red this time, but he saw the quick breath she took and how the slightest tinge of pink started to creep up from under the white silk blouse.

He'd noticed when she came in that her shoes were worn, not terribly, but they were old, and the suit was a little faded from time, so it was obvious she needed this job. Could he trust her with it, though?

"I'm honest, hard-working, and always on time." She repeated the qualities as if she'd memorized them in high school during one of the many classes kids had to take on how to get through job interviews, or in her college days, perhaps. If she hadn't lied about the college days, that is.

"Every person in an interview says that, Ms. Miller. Tell me who you really are. You've answered all of my questions on the questionnaire with a great deal of confidence and ability, what gave you those strengths?"

He leaned a little closer, turned the charm up another notch with a smile that invited trust and confidence, and gave her a quick conspiratorial wink. That flustered her even more and she shifted around in her seat a little. But she showed how good she was under pressure and gave a logical answer.

"I was raised by a strong mother and I was in cheerleading throughout high school. Oh, and at the university too." That last part was added quickly, but he let it slide. She was obviously playing a game, a game she needed to win, or she wouldn't be here. "I learned how to be a part of a team, how to smile even when it hurts, and that all that matters is reaching your goals. It helped to boost my confidence and it's something I've never lost sight of, how my mother raised me and my experiences as I grew up."

He'd already decided to hire her, if for no other reason than to watch her squirm. She'd started to ramble a little and she knew it. He could see the panic in her eyes but let her go on.

"I did charity work at school too, and I guess I've just learned over the years to be a strong person. To go after what I want, to make sure I excel at whatever I do, and to make sure I'm the right person for the job."

He sat back and nodded, impressed with how she'd pulled it back from a ramble to a solid answer. Not bad.

"Good. And can you explain to me what you are hoping for from this job?" Another throwaway question, but as he looked at her suit again, noticed how the jacket was frayed at the bottom hem, he was suddenly very interested. How had she come to be in this situation?

Oh, he knew about the divorce and the alleged job she'd lost, but what happened to her parents? Couldn't she rely on them for support?

"I've never asked for a handout in my life." She began, but stopped and took a deep breath. "Not that I'm implying you were, but I've always worked hard for what I have."

Something about her told him that wasn't quite true

either. Batting your pretty, long eyelashes wasn't hard work.

"I'm in a bad place now, I need a job, but I'm hoping I get more than that." She hurried to add more when he leaned back with an 'I knew it' smile spread all over his face. "I mean, I'm looking for something that I can make a career out of. I'm only in my 20s, so I have a lot of time to invest into a job where I will spend a lot of the hours of my life. I'm looking for a future, not just a job."

Another solid answer, he thought with another nod. "Good. When can you start?"

"Today, if need be." She said with a smile that would melt glaciers.

"No, not today. Let's see, these are the benefits of the position." He handed her a paper with a list he'd drawn up previously. "The apartment is near to work, so you won't even have to worry about catching the bus, you can walk if you want to, but you'll also have a company car, after proof of a driving license is provided, of course."

"That's the salary?" She asked, clearly blown away by the figure. It wasn't that much over what other similar positions offered in the area, but that on top of an apartment and a company car was a lot to offer.

"Yes. The apartment will be paid for by the company, I need you close and available at a moment's notice. This isn't just a position where you'll go home after 5 pm and the job ends. You'll have to be available 24 hours a day, 7 days a week, Keily." He looked at her, staring deep into her eyes to try to gauge her reaction. When she only smiled more brightly, he carried on. "You'll have little downtime. Can you handle that?"

"Of course, I can!" She said immediately. "When do you want me to start?"

"In a week. Get moved into the apartment, there's a car in the parking lot waiting for you if you need it to move from…wherever you are right now, and all of the utilities are on. The Wi-Fi password is on the back of the router in the apartment. It's in the living room, by the way." Something else he'd had arranged before he came over, his PA in California had arranged it all. She was there now, working with Wally. "Assuming your criminal background check comes back clean."

He'd added that just to watch her squirm. He already knew she was clean, and he wouldn't press the issue of her previous employment or her education. For now.

"That shouldn't be a problem." She turned her head away a little, only a fraction of an inch, but enough to tell him that what he'd said had made her nervous.

Something about the woman intrigued him, but maybe it wasn't simply her history as a cheerleader. Maybe it was who she was, the unattainable former wife of a quarterback, a guy that was supposed to have it all but ended up with nothing because he'd busted his knee while he was still in school. He'd read about it all, how her husband had lost his chance, how he'd ended up working at a news station instead of being a star football player. Yes, he knew it all, and maybe it was just a little sadistic of him, but he wanted her for one main reason.

She'd been one of the kinds of girls that would torture him back when he was in high school here, the kind that would tease and taunt him, but would never ever date him. And now, she wanted what he had to offer. She was all but begging for it, in fact. He'd have loved to have Keily in this position back when he was an awkward kid, just trying to get through high school so he could get on with the rest of his life. He'd wanted a friend, a companion, someone to tell him he mattered, but girls like her? They only wanted to be cruel to him.

Well, fun-time had only just begun for him. He'd make sure he didn't sink the company or cause a problem that would bring charges against him, but he would make sweet, lovely Ms. Miller earn her pay. Every last dime of it.

"I guess that's all then." He leaned forward again. "If you can let me have your driver's license and the other pertinent information, we'll get started on everything."

She handed over everything he asked for and as he typed everything into his laptop, he realized he hadn't asked her anything really important, like how many words she could type, if she would agree to a confidentiality agreement, or if she could even prove she could read. He glanced back at her, saw the confident smile she gave him, and knew she was bluffing her way through this.

He sent the information from her driver's license off to his insurance company to add to the company car, and then added her information into the company database for employees. His PA back in California would sort out the rest of it.

"Okay, good, here's the keys to the car. You're on the insurance now, they've approved you, and this is the paper you'll need to keep in your car." He pulled the paper from the printer behind his desk and then pulled out the next one, the rental agreement for the house, the confidentiality agreement, and a few more forms she had to sign, like her employment contract. "I need you to sign these."

He explained each form to her and then made copies for her. "Well, then, I guess I'll see you in a week."

"You will."

"Oh, one more thing." He opened his desk drawer and took out a small box. "This is your work phone. It's already set up, in a protective case, and will be another thing we provide for you. It's only for work."

She took out the new iPhone and stared at it. It was the top-of-the-line, latest edition of the awfully expensive phone.

"Make sure you turn it on and have it ready for your first day. I'll be up at 5 am. I expect you here at 7 am, 8 at the latest if I have you pick up anything first. Until then, enjoy your time off before you start. Welcome to the company."

He smiled as she walked away, her head high and her back straight. She was quiet though, so maybe she hadn't expected it all. She wasn't expecting what she was about to get either, but that could wait. All of it could wait, because in one week's time, he'd have the head cheerleader, former wife of the quarterback, as his personal assistant. She'd have to answer to his every beck and call. Life had suddenly become remarkably interesting.

"Goodbye, see you in a week, Mr. Sinclair." She called out as she left the office. She probably thought it was her due, everything he'd just given her, people like her always thought life owed them something. She was about to find out how very untrue that was.

5

Keily

*V*iolet was going to eat her words, Keily couldn't help but think as she left the building, a cocky swing to her hips as she walked along the parking lot. She'd just been offered far more than she could have asked for, and she'd have to work for it, but so what? She'd proven her sister wrong and that was so worth anything she'd have to put up with.

There were two cars there, one that was obviously his, a Cadillac that got her attention, and one that was obviously meant for her. A black sedan of the more utilitarian variety sat beside it. She saw a gold medallion on the back of the car in the shape of the company logo and smiled.

She'd got the job and so much more! Excitement

bubbled through her as she hit the button and the car doors unlocked. She slid into the leather seat and looked at the interior of the car. It might be domestic, but he hadn't skimped on the features. Leather, top-of-the-range heated seats, and a sound system that also served as a GPS system with phone syncing capabilities. It had it all and she ran her hand over the passenger seat with a grin she could feel on her face.

What was the apartment like? He'd said it was just down the street. She dragged her handbag up from the passenger side floor where she'd thrown it and dug out the paper that served as her rental agreement. She found the address, typed it into the GPS panel, and pulled out of the parking lot.

She saw the place before the voice of the GPS came over the speakers. It was an apartment complex with two units side-by-side to create twelve apartments. She saw a communal pool, a building that apparently contained a sauna, and then her apartment. It really wasn't that far from the office, less than a mile and a half. Too far to walk in heels, she thought, but she could wear loafers or running shoes then change before she got into the office.

But why do that when she had a car?

"Violet's going to shit herself," Keily said out loud with a smirk as she got out of the car. The place was quiet, sheltered by tall palmetto trees, and on the expensive side. Far more than she could have afforded on her own.

She opened the door with the only other key on the keyring Logan gave her. It wasn't a large apartment, bigger than Violet's but not as huge as her house. A small foyer opened into the living room on the left and a kitchen on the right. Down a short hallway, she found two bedrooms, a bathroom, and at the back door, she found a utility room for storage, and a small area with privacy fencing to give her a space of her own.

The place was empty, but in the kitchen, she found all the appliances she'd need from a fridge to a stove and dishwasher. Hidden behind what she thought was a closet door she found a washer and dryer. Keily wanted to dance, to laugh with the thrill of it as she ran her hands over the black tiles that covered the back walls of the kitchen and the black marble of the counters.

Cherrywood cabinets both overhead and below the countertops lined the back wall. An island in the middle held a sink and a dishwasher with a large prep area. Towards the front was an empty area where she'd put a table and chairs, there in front of the window, she decided.

All the beautiful furniture she'd bought when she and Joe were married had been sold with the house, but she'd find something, even if it took her some time. She'd buy one thing at a time if she had to. It wasn't like she had anyone to entertain, after all. All her former friends had drifted off as her finances dwindled and her sister was always busy.

Her parents might come over, but she doubted it. They tended to stay home, out of their children's lives now that they were grown. But maybe they had a bed she could take off their hands, she wondered as she walked back to the master bedroom. She found another surprise there; her own bathroom with a black tiled shower, a sink with a lit mirror over it, and a toilet.

Nothing was cheap or poorly made, it was all more than she could have ever dreamed of. She'd move in tonight if she had a bed to sleep on, just to get out of Violet's place. She'd hung her handbag on a peg on the wall in the foyer, but she ran back to dig around in it when she heard an unfamiliar sound screeching inside.

She swiped at the screen until it answered, and brought the phone to her ear. She'd seen Logan's name on the display and dread made her throat tight when she said hello. Had he found out she was a fake already and was calling to demand she bring the keys and the car back?

"Hello, Keily?" His deep voice so close to her ear sent a shiver down her spine, and she looked back into the apartment with sadness. He must have found out something, he sounded so stern.

"Hello, Mr. Sinclair, what can I do for you?" She tried

to force confidence into her voice and hoped he didn't hear the slight shake she couldn't prevent.

"Have you found the apartment yet?" He asked smoothly, his voice less stern.

"Yes, it's very nice, thank you." She answered, a little confused as to why he would call her if he hadn't found out her resume was completely made up. She leaned back against the white steel door, obviously meant for security, and waited.

"Good. There's a laptop in the closet in the living room I forgot to mention. Also, everything looks good and I'm going to go ahead and put you on the payroll. You'll have a sign-on bonus in your checking account in about an hour."

"A what?" She had no idea what that was. She'd given him her banking information as part of the paperwork she'd signed earlier so wasn't surprised about that, but she was about the bonus.

"A sign-on bonus, companies often give them to new employees to help the employee get settled in and as an incentive to, well, sign on with the company." He sounded baffled that she didn't know what it was. "Anyway, check the account in an hour or so, it should be there."

"Of course, Mr. Sin..." but he didn't let her finish.

"And please, call me Logan. My last name is a mouthful and you will probably be saying it a lot."

"Of course, Mr.. uh, Logan." She smiled to herself, her voice going a little softer. Almost a purr.

She barely knew him, and he'd already given her so much. He was a very handsome man with strong features and a voice that definitely kept her attention. She would spend a lot of time with him if she was lucky enough to keep the job, maybe one day they could make it more than a work relationship.

For now, she'd keep it platonic she decided, until she knew more about him.

"Have a nice day, Keily. Settle in, take your time, and be ready to come in to work soon. I'll need you." He chuckled at the end as if he'd made a joke.

She laughed back, not sure what was so funny, but already she knew it would be what he wanted to hear. She'd learned that with Joe, give a man what he wants, even trivial things like a laugh, and you'd soon have him eating out of your hand.

"Thank you, Logan. See you soon." She knew she should probably gush over how generous he'd been, but he didn't seem like the kind that would like gushing women. Women that laughed at his bad jokes, maybe, but not gushers.

She went into the living room once he ended the call and found the closet. Inside there was a laptop sitting on top of a box. She took it out, and filled with curiosity, sat down on the floor and typed in her bank details. Her mouth dropped when she saw how much she now had in her account.

Holy fuck. She knew a used furniture store not far away; she could pay them to bring the furniture today if she left now. Quickly, she put the laptop back in the closet, locked the place up, and sped off in the direction of the store. Within twenty minutes of arriving she'd picked out a couch, coffee table, a bed, a recliner, and a table set for the kitchen. It wasn't new stuff, and it wasn't expensive, but they'd deliver it by 5 pm, the store manager assured her.

Every piece had been cleaned and sanitized and would suit her for now. A black velvet sectional sofa and an oak coffee table would go in the living room, along with the black velvet recliner. The queen-sized bed was basically a simple frame with a new mattress, the tags were still on the mattress it was so new, and someone had just decided to get rid of it. That surprised her, but she didn't question it. Later, she'd find a headboard for it, but right now, she needed to get to a department store.

By the time she arrived home she had food, drinks, everything she'd need for the kitchen, household goods like small appliances and curtains, sheets and a new comforter set, pillows, new clothes, as well as makeup. There was also a new smart television that she'd be able to watch with a dinner she'd order later from a place that delivered. Despite everything she'd spent, she'd still barely put a dent in the amount Logan had given her.

The furniture was delivered and set up by 7:30 pm and she had ordered some Chinese food for dinner. While she waited for the food to arrive, she decided to call her sister. She'd paid her phone bill, so she used her own phone to call Violet.

"Where are you, Keily? Hiding out at the bar again?" Violet's tired voice came over the line with no enthusiasm at all.

"Why would you think I was there?" Keily shot back, her hackles up already. Why didn't Violet have any faith in her? Why did she have to be so damned negative?

"Well, you aren't home, it's 7:30, and you had an interview today. I assume you blew it and you're down there at the bar begging men to buy you drinks again." The sneer in Violet's voice only made Keily angrier.

"No, I'm not at the bar, thank you very much. I got the job, for your information. Thanks for the support, by the way, it really helped my confidence this morning."

"You what?" It sounded like Violet dropped her phone but quickly picked it back up again. "Did you say you got the job?"

"Yes, I did, and not only that, I got a company car, an apartment, a sign-on bonus and all sorts."

"Keily, you didn't, uh, sleep with the guy, did you?"

Violet's voice was filled with disapproval and Keily was certain she'd have a stroke she was so angry.

"No, dammit. How could you say something like that? Fucking hell, Violet. I know we've had our differences but that was just pure bitch, right there." Keily almost hung up the phone, but Violet stopped her.

"I'm sorry, I'm just tired." There was an emphasis on the word tired that made Keily's eyes narrow. She would have let it go, but she felt like it was yet another dig, not a real apology.

"I can't believe you. Fine, I'll send you pictures. Or a video. Hang on, I'll call you on WhatsApp." Keily hung up the phone, added her sister's contact information to the app, and called right back. This time with video. "So, this is my new home."

Violet's face went slack, and her mouth dropped open as Keily used the back camera on her phone to pan around the kitchen. She walked out to the living room.

"Wow. It was furnished?" Violet asked and Kiely laughed.

"No, I bought all that this afternoon." She made sure to get a view of the black satin curtains with lace panels that added to the chic look she'd wanted to give the place. She'd worked hard and quickly to get everything arranged.

The television hung on the wall opposite the couch and she got a shot of that too before she moved through the rest of the house. Then she finished off by going outside to show her jealous sister her new car.

"Keily, are you sure you didn't…" Her voice trailed off. "How did you get that job?"

"I did well with the interview, what can I say?" It felt good to rub something in Violet's face for a change. Keily had been down on her luck for so long now that it was nice to get back that familiar, superior feeling.

"You must have. So, you aren't coming home tonight?" Violet asked, sounding a little happier about that than Keily cared for.

"I am home," Keily answered waspishly.

"Okay, okay, don't get your panties in a knot. When are you going to pick up your things?"

"Tomorrow, I guess. I don't start for a week, so I'll have time to get used to everything." Keily went back into the house, closed the door and locked it, then went to sprawl out on the couch she'd sprayed down thoroughly with disinfectant, just to be safe.

"You'd better take a crash course on being a PA or you'll get fired and be right back here with me," Violet told her.

"I know that. Besides, I did the same thing for Joe for years, it's not that hard." Keily answered, totally confident in her ability to fake it until she had it down pat.

"Mmhmm. I won't give your room away right away, then." Violet answered.

"Why do you have to undermine me like that?" Keily huffed, but Violet apologized, for real this time.

"Really, I'm happy for you. I wish you all the best of luck and congratulations." Her sister kindly answered.

"Thank you. Oh, my food's here, talk to you later, bye." She hung up as a knock came at the front door.

She paid the woman at the door, took the food, and placed it on the island. She took down one of her new plain white plates from the cabinet, a few bowls, and emptied the boxes of food into each. She pulled a bottle of wine from the fridge and after she carried everything to the table and sat down, she picked up the full glass and toasted herself on a job well done. Now, if she could pull off the actual job, she'd be an incredibly happy lady. And if she could get Logan into her bed eventually? Even better.

6

Logan

*L*ogan sipped a cup of coffee and glanced at his watch. He stood in his kitchen and it was now 6:30 am exactly. Time to get to work, he decided. Today was Keily's first day and he planned to put her through the wringer.

The idea had grown over the seven days since she first walked into his office. In quiet moments, of which there were many as he prepared to open the factory and office, he'd started to make notes. He had an entire file on his computer of things he planned to do to make her miserable. He'd named the file 'breaking the cheerleader', which was a silly name for a document file, but fuck it.

By the time he arrived at the office, he'd finished a

morning workout, had breakfast, worked on some paperwork for the California factory, and had fired a supervisor that had taken it upon himself to falsify workers timestamps and add their hours to his. Wally didn't know how the man had done it, the whole thing was accomplished with software the man shouldn't have had access to, but it had happened, so it was being investigated. The police were involved because it was fraud, and Logan might have to go back to California for a little while. It was a bad time to leave South Carolina, but if it had to be done, he'd go.

He took the elevator up to the third floor after he greeted the new security guard and put on another pot of coffee. He took out his phone and texted Keily with an order for coffee and doughnuts from a place that was out of her way. She promptly agreed and sent the order back to him to acknowledge she understood.

It was one of the busiest places in the mornings because they were only open for a short time, long enough to sell the day's batches of doughnuts, then they'd close. He didn't eat the sweet treats, but it was all part of his plan. With a smile, he started to take out the stacks of files he'd created from the job applications he'd received already.

By the time he finished the stack on her desk was two feet tall and wobbled quite a bit. The applications ranged from people that wanted to work in the factory to office staff and department heads. It wasn't really her job to hire anyone, but she could whittle the pile down, as he instructed in the note he placed on top of the files.

"Good morning." She called out when she walked in thirty minutes later on a breeze of citrus perfume. She was all sauntering hips, a self-satisfied grin, and eyes that were full of challenge. "How are you?"

"You're late," Logan replied with a hint of censure in his voice.

Dressed in a new red pencil skirt with black heels, and a tight red blouse, Keily stopped in her tracks with a large bag on her shoulder. It probably held the laptop he'd arranged for her and her personal things. That didn't matter though, not to him. His eyes focused on her hands. She carried a cardboard tray with coffee and the bag of doughnuts between her dainty hands. She blinked at him quickly, her gray eyes full of consternation.

"Pardon?" She stood there in the waiting area of the outer office obviously unsure of what to do next.

"You were meant to be here ten minutes ago. You're now late and it's your first day. Not a good sign, Keily."

"But you wanted coffee and doughnuts." She sputtered, rancor knitting her brows together. When he tilted his head, sending his own challenge with his stance, she took a deep breath and lifted her head to look him in the eye. "I'm sorry, it won't happen again."

"No, it won't, or you'll be out of a job." She hadn't moved from her spot in the front of the office, so he walked over to take the coffee from her. He pulled the top off and looked down at it. "What's this?"

"The coffee with two creams and sugar that you asked for." She repeated back the coffee order he'd sent to her.

"I don't have sugar in my coffee. Take it back, get another one."

"But they've closed now." She protested as he walked away without even taking the doughnuts.

"Pardon?" He repeated her earlier question. He turned to face her, his face a mask of stern reproach. "What did you say?"

"I, oh, um, I'll find something downstairs for you."

"See that you do." He turned back to head to his office, but he heard the way she sighed with resignation.

Good, don't complain, just get on with your job, he thought with a smirk. Use some of those skills you learned on the cheerleading squad and pretend you're enjoying yourself. Take one for the team and all that nonsense.

She hadn't noticed the smell of coffee in the office, or if she had, she hadn't mentioned it, he noted as he poured another cup and sat behind his desk. She'd left the other cup of coffee and the doughnuts on a small table placed between two small chairs in the reception area. He frowned and wrote out another sticky note.

"Throw this away, why did you leave it here? We don't have a full janitorial staff yet. Don't leave your trash lying around." He went out and stuck it on the top of the coffee he'd ordered.

She'd got the order exactly right, but that wasn't the point. Humiliating her was.

The way he'd been humiliated by women like her all those years ago. He remembered so many instances of humiliation, when his mother had put a gap in his hair with the hair clippers, the way the cheerleaders had snickered and sneered when he'd been given aftershave on his 17th birthday and they'd laughed and made snide comments because it was apparently something cheap, but all his grandfather could afford. He'd gone into the school that day, certain that he smelled like a man, even felt a little confident for a change, but that had changed the minute one of the cheerleaders caught a whiff of him. He'd never worn the aftershave again, but he still had the bottle.

He'd kept it as a reminder to himself that it didn't matter what something cost, gifts were made out of love. He could now afford the most expensive aftershave on the market, but that didn't matter. That bottle still went with him wherever he roamed.

The door to his office was open when she came back in, carrying a new cup of coffee. "I've got a new cup…"

Her words trailed off as she spotted the cup of coffee on his desk and looked around until she found the coffee pot. Irritation pinched at the corners of her lips and eyes, but she just plastered on a smile and brought the coffee to his desk. "Here you go."

"Thank you." He said dismissively and turned his head away from her. "I've left a few things on your desk. Can you look through them and get back to me by lunchtime with something?"

"Of course, Logan, whatever you need." She left the office immediately, without further complaint, and he smiled when he heard her quiet, but certainly colorful, reaction to the mound of files on her desk. She hadn't noticed them then.

"How the fuck, what the fuck is this?" She said very quietly, but he had excellent hearing. "By fucking lunchtime? Fuck."

His smile turned into a grin as he listened to her outside the office. He also heard when she discovered the note on the coffee cup she'd left sitting on the table. She'd been at her desk for a half-hour when he heard her chair slide away from her desk and she walked over to the cup. "Well fuck. Okay, so I forgot the coffee here, sue me."

She was feisty and as much as he hated to admit it, he

liked that about her. Unfortunately for her, she was about to learn that feisty wasn't always a good thing. It came from a place that generated over-confidence and a sense of entitlement to the better things in life, based solely on the idea that you were born perfect and deserved them.

Logan had spent his entire youth thinking he deserved to be treated like scum and he'd learned to try to be invisible. His place in life was at the bottom, but surprisingly, the longer he spent in his room studying, reading, researching, and learning, the better off he became. He won awards at school for his efforts, awards that led to scholarships, and he'd graduated from his university with no debt at all, but with a powerful education that had brought him to where he was today.

And she had…what? A job as a personal assistant. Well done, cheerleader.

"Keily, I need you to answer that phone." He called into the office just before midday, the ringing incessant as she ignored it.

"Excuse me?" She called out.

"Answer the damn phone, what do you think your job is?" His voice rose as he called back out to her; annoyance high at her complete lack of thought. She'd let two phone calls ring until he'd finally answered them himself. This was her third and last chance.

He heard her pick up and answer the call, only to

reply that the caller had dialed the wrong number. Well, it wasn't important at least. Her tone could use some improvement though. He made a note on a legal pad he'd taken out to write such things down on.

She'd been given a complete list of her job duties, but he'd retained the right to add to those duties as part of her contract. Hadn't she even bothered to read that during the week he'd given her to prepare? He wondered with frustration.

He got up from the desk and looked out the door. She was on her personal phone, and the files he'd given her to look through had barely been touched.

"What are you doing?" He asked with ice in his voice.

"Sorry, my sister texted me and I needed to answer her."

"You did? And what else have you been doing? You've barely made it through those files at all."

"Oh, I've been reading through the files and answering emails." She told him and looked up at him with a haughty shake of her head.

"What emails?" He asked carefully.

"The ones from applicants looking for a job." She replied and showed him her computer screen. There was a desktop computer under her desk and the monitor was on, showing the company website's emails.

"How did you get into that?" He stared at her,

stunned because she wasn't supposed to be able to get into that section of the website.

"Oh, the sign-in information was in the job description and duties you gave me."

"It was?" He went to the desk and looked down to see she had the job description folder turned to page two.

"Yes, it says I'm to answer the emails." She looked at him with an expression that could only be described as...attitude.

"That shouldn't be in there. Close out of that and don't sign into that part of the website ever again." He'd have to contact the PA in California and ask her what the hell she'd been thinking when she'd added that information in. He barely knew this woman in front of him, she shouldn't have that kind of access yet. "Stop answering emails and do what you've been told to do."

He left her to go back to his office and stew for a while. Okay, so she had been doing part of her job, according to the description, but still, she shouldn't have been allowed that access and now she was behind on what he'd assigned her to do.

He was so irritated he decided to go to lunch early.

"I'm going out. Answer the phone, go through that pile and find me someone decent to hire in the HR department, and then I guess you can go to lunch." He was almost at the door when her voice stopped him.

"But it'll be hours before I get through this pile." She

protested, her eyes shooting fire at him before she extinguished it.

"Then you should have brought your lunch in to have at your desk. Order something and have it delivered. Think on your feet, Keily. Really, can't you think for yourself at all?" He shook his head in disgust and left the office, after locking his own door securely.

He didn't hear her response and didn't care if she'd even made one. He went out for an hour. An hour in which his thoughts kept turning to her, to that tight red skirt, and how much he'd like to bend her over her desk and pull that skirt up around her hips. She looked like the kind that wore a thong, he decided over a glass of wine with a gourmet lunch.

She likely wore black lace, cradled between the pale globes of her ass, and stockings with black garters. But he'd noted she didn't have any kind of stockings on at all, so maybe just the panties, he thought. By the time he made it back to work, he'd lectured himself on fantasizing about employees, even if they were beautiful.

She was just a checkmark on a long list of people he wanted to crush under his shoe. Not the best business plan, but she was the only person he'd hired. The rest he'd find other ways to crush. Simply by buying the house and the factory, he'd already shown who had the power in this town that time was on the verge of forgetting.

Manufacturing had started to move overseas decades ago, leaving towns impoverished and without much hope of a resurgence of those glory days. He'd give hope back to the people of this town, even if he had to charge more for his products. Unlike some manufacturers that moved their plants overseas and still charged huge markups, his markups would go to his employees, not to shareholders. By the time it was all said and done, he'd be a savior to the town that had rejected him in his youth.

As he walked back into the office a little while later, he saw that she was quietly looking over files, a mess on her desk from the lunch she'd ordered. She was feisty, independent, and able to buckle down when she needed to, but she was also messy.

"Clean that shit off your desk, Keily. You aren't at home, you're in *my* office, and I won't tolerate a mess."

"Excuse me?" She started, but then looked down and threw the empty burger box, and French fry box away. She loudly sucked the last dregs of her drink through her straw, then very deliberately threw it away while she held his gaze. "All gone."

"Thank you." He looked at the piles of folders on her desk and lifted an eyebrow. "Well?"

"These are HR possibilities, these are office staff, and these are department heads." There were three small piles on her left. The much larger pile on her right was soon explained. "These are definitely not good for any of those positions."

"Good. Thanks." He picked up the three piles and then waved at the others. "Shred those then throw them away."

"Yes, Logan." She'd have to go to another room to shred the applications, the central supply room for this floor, but there was a phone in there if she needed to answer it.

He smiled as she walked out of the office. Not so high and mighty now, was she?

He wrote a few emails to her with instructions for the next day, each task more impossible than the last, and set them to send at different times in the middle of the night. He'd instructed her not to turn off notifications during the night in case he needed her urgently. In between those, he wrote other emails that reviewed her skills and nitpicked the minutest thing he'd taken note of. They should wake her up at regular intervals. She definitely wouldn't be so superior tomorrow; she'd be too damned tired.

7

Keily

"Let me get this straight, you were given a car, an apartment, a new phone, laptop, and all your expenses are paid for? And you really think this man only wants you to be his PA?" Violet's voice grated on Keily's nerves exactly one week after she'd started to work for Logan.

Keily stared at her sister as she gathered up the last of her things from around Violet's place. "Yes, that's all he wants, a PA there to answer his every beck and call."

"Yeah, right." Violet snorted. "You'll see, soon enough, he'll try to get in your panties, and you'll know I was right."

"Excuse me?" Keily turned around and stared at her sister. "Are you really implying that the only reason

Logan hired me was to become his mistress or something?"

"What else do you have to offer him? Your typing skills suck, you don't know the first thing about computer software, and you've never worked a day in your life." Violet paused but started back in before Keily could answer. "And no, cheerleading doesn't count. The same way playing tennis doesn't count, it was your exercise, not a job."

Violet hadn't been a cheerleader and Keily had always thought her sister was jealous over that, now she knew she was. "If that's how you feel about me, dear sister, I'll leave you to your perfect life then."

"Don't come crying to me when you find out I was right, Keily. I've had enough of your bragging and your holier-than-thou attitude. Frankly, I can't afford to take care of you anymore, anyway, so sink or swim, *dear sister.*" Violet stood there with her arms crossed in front of her chest, her face pulled down in a frown of distaste.

"Enough of my bragging? Oh, that's it." Keily grabbed a shoe she'd been looking for that had somehow ended up under her sister's couch and stormed out of the house.

It had been a week from hell and this was the final straw. Keily threw the items she'd picked up from Violet's into the back of her car and drove back to her apartment, alone. It was almost 7 pm, she'd order dinner tonight she decided.

The last week had been brutal and a lesson in utter humiliation. As Violet had noted, Keily was a terrible typist, could barely figure out how to open Word documents, and had no idea how to open, or create, PDF files. Logan had spent at least a half-hour of every day upbraiding her over how terrible she was at everything. Only today, he'd figured out she was Googling just about every task he'd given her to do.

Now, she was at home, with a bottle of red wine, wiping tears from her face as her Chinese food grew cold on the table. She'd had such high hopes for this job, but she wasn't sure how long she could take Logan's demands. Her phone vibrated on the table and she stared at it with something close to hatred.

It was her work phone and she knew it would be Logan calling.

"What are you doing?" His voice demanded when she accepted the call.

"I'm having dinner, Logan. What can I do for you?" She stared at the now congealed sesame chicken and decided to heat it up in the microwave.

"You didn't finish the report on the meetings I have scheduled for this week. I told you, I need a page of bullet points for each meeting, who they are, what reason the meeting is for, and what key points I need to remember about each person the meeting is with."

She wanted to say *that's because you came in with a pile of advertising agencies you wanted me to research*, but she kept it to herself. "I'll do them this evening, Logan, I'm sorry. I did print out a report of the ad agencies though."

"Yes, I see a few typos in there too, Keily. Are you sure you actually went to any classes at this university you went to? And what did you do at this other place you worked at? Because you're not particularly good at this at all."

She wanted to burst into tears, but she dug her new acrylic nails into her palm and bit back the words she wanted to say. "I'll do better tomorrow, Logan. I'm sorry."

"Fine. But I'm telling you now, if you don't shape up soon, you're out of a job, and out of the rest of it too."

"I'm, well…" she spluttered, unsure of what to say. She really needed this job now, even if Logan was an absolute dick. An attractive one, but still a dick.

"Just don't make me regret my decision, okay?" He finally huffed before he hung up.

For a moment, she hung her head, then she went into the bathroom and dug around in her makeup kit under the sink until she found a nail file. She hated to admit it, but the decision to splurge on long stiletto nails was a stupid idea. She could barely type with her nails at a short length, trying to type with one-inch long nails was all but impossible. She'd have to file them down.

An hour later, she looked at the pile of acrylic dust on her table and wanted to cry. The nails had been so pretty, so expensive, but now, she'd be able to get back to her normal speed. She pulled up the file on her laptop after she cleared away the dust, went to the cloud where she'd learned to keep the files she'd send to Logan, and started to work on the report he'd asked for. It took another hour, and by the time she'd finished, showered, and changed into her pajamas, it was after 10 pm.

A notification dinged on her phone. Which wouldn't be so bad, if she could turn her notifications off when she went to bed. She heard every single time her phone buzzed during the night and she was running on fumes. To make matters worse, she had to coordinate with the PA in California too, and they were hours behind the South Carolina plant. She'd have to get up and check the emails because sometimes she'd have to respond to them quickly.

Her eyes nearly crossed when she saw Logan's latest email. He wanted her to get up at 5 am, drive two hours away, and buy him a pair of black socks from a specific store in Charleston. Why the hell couldn't he get socks from Sears or somewhere at the mall? But this was Logan Sinclair, so there was no fucking way he'd wear department store socks, oh no. He'd have fucking boutique socks, or he'd have her head.

Keily was tired, more tired than she'd ever been in her life, and she just wanted a complete night's sleep. She'd thought she'd get a break over the weekend, but that was a pipe dream that had gone off like a pipe bomb. He'd kept her busy all weekend with responding to emails from suppliers and buyers, arranging meetings, and now he wanted her to get up early, drive for four hours roundtrip, and get back to work by 9:30 am. For a pair of socks.

She nearly screamed. She nearly wrote him an email to tell him to take his job and shove it, but she'd had that argument with Violet and knew she had nowhere else to go. Logan's little tantrums about getting the wrong coffee, or ordering his lunch at the wrong time, and the way he screamed at her when she did something wrong, would all have to be put up with.

There was nowhere else for her to go, no other job that would provide her with the benefits that Logan did. He might be the world's biggest jerk, but he more than paid for it. So what if Violet thought he only wanted to sleep with her? She hadn't seen the slightest clue of that, not really. Sometimes, she'd catch him looking at her oddly, as if he was thinking something intense about her, but then the look would disappear.

He'd shown far more interest in the black-haired

human resources director named Rosa he'd hired than he had in her. Keily couldn't blame him, though, the woman was stunning, with long tanned legs, dark brown sensual eyes, and a flair for dressing that even outdid Keily's level of sophistication. Despite the fact that the woman was beautiful, with a slim figure, a heart-shaped face and a nose some women would pay surgeons to have for themselves, Keily liked her.

She was good at her job, spoke kindly to Keily, and coordinated with her to get both their jobs done. She'd asked Keily out for a drink earlier that day, but Keily had refused. She didn't want to admit she was too tired to go out, or afraid she'd get interrupted by another demand from Logan, so she'd asked for a raincheck. Rosa had accepted the refusal with a smile and a pat on Keily's arm.

That pat had nearly brought her to tears and she'd excused herself to go to the ladies' room. Over the last few months, there hadn't been anyone who'd touched her with kindness, not like that. Sure, it was a throw-away gesture, but it was also just...really nice. Especially after putting up with Logan all week.

By the time the weekend rolled around, Keily was certain that Logan was picking on her on purpose. Even when she showed him the text messages to prove he'd asked for whatever she brought him, he'd dismiss it and say she should have known what he meant. The drive to get the socks? He told her he'd changed his mind *after* she'd driven the two hours to get down to Charleston. He'd just order the socks online because he was going away for the weekend anyway. He had to go to California to take care of some business over there.

She thought his weekend away would mean no texts, no emails, no Logan, but she'd been wrong. She'd invited Rosa over for lunch and was about to take the salmon off the grill outside and bring it in when her phone buzzed. Rosa had just come out with two glasses of white wine and a smile when she heard Keily's work phone buzz.

"Him again?" She asked and Keily nodded.

"Always." With a sigh, she looked at the phone, breathed in deeply with her eyes closed for a minute, then sent Logan the same file she'd already sent him three times that day. "He can't seem to get the file to open, even though I've not changed it."

"I think he's just messing with you, honey," Rosa answered and helped her by taking the salmon off the grill before it started to burn. "Come inside, let's eat, and forget about him for a little while."

"I've sent it to him in another format, maybe that will work," Keily answered and followed her new friend into the kitchen of the apartment. "Thanks for coming over, by the way, it's nice to have some company for a change."

"It's my pleasure. I'm new in town and I have to admit, it's been a little lonely without anyone I know here." Rosa, in a pair of dark olive-green shorts that hit her midthigh and a black tank-top, looked the picture of sophistication, even in such a simple outfit.

Keily had on a pair of white capri pants and a floral top, paired with strappy sandals. She wasn't looking too bad herself, she thought, even if she'd had to use extra concealer under her eyes this morning to hide the dark circles that had formed there. And the clothes had come from a consignment shop. She might have a few extra pennies in her bank account, and she might have walked through the shop with her head down and her hair hiding her face, but she'd already started to learn; save for the hard times.

"You came down from Charlotte, didn't you?" Keily asked and pulled a salad to go with the light lunch from the fridge.

"Yes, after my husband and I split up, North Carolina just wasn't doing it for me anymore. I grew up in a small town, way out in the sticks, and moved to Charlotte with him when I got my first job. After the divorce, well, I needed a change. Logan offered me a job, so here I am." She smiled with her hands up in the air as she sat down and scooted her chair a little closer to the table.

"I wish I'd thought of that when my husband and I split up. Just leave here and start somewhere new." Keily sighed as she put salad on her plate and looked up at Rosa. "I guess I was too afraid to leave everything I knew. You're brave, I like that."

"Thanks. It is scary, but, well, it's turned out good so far." Rosa put a bite of salmon into her mouth and her eyes closed with pleasure. "That is so good."

"I'm glad you like it. Grilling is a secret hobby of mine." Keily smiled ruefully as memories flooded back. "I started on a charcoal grill one day. My husband was, um, sick, and I wanted grilled pork chops. You wouldn't believe how long it took me to get that charcoal lit and going."

"I would! I used to do it for my family when I was in high school." Rosa grinned and Keily took another bite of her food.

Joe's illness had been self-inflicted, a hangover to beat all hangovers. The blurry eyes and stench of stale alcohol were something she'd started to get used to, but still hated, the longer they were married. He'd barely been able to lift his head off the pillow, so she'd decided to grill by herself. The only problem had been, she didn't know how. Once she got the hang of it, she found she enjoyed sitting outside, waiting for her meal to cook.

Once the meal was finished and the dishes washed, they went back out to the small garden area, another glass of wine in hand. For the first time in a week, Keily had started to relax as the wine began to flood into her veins, and the giddy feeling it gave her was nice. The soft strains of her favorite country music drifted softly from the kitchen while she pondered the strangeness of having a friend to talk with, and a nice quiet evening to enjoy. She contemplated the even stranger knowledge that there was money in her bank account because she'd earned it.

"I'm going to have to call a cab to get home," Rosa said with a soft giggle. "This wine is delicious."

"I have another bottle, don't worry," Keily assured her and then looked over at Rosa, in the other sun lounger that matched the one Keily was settled in. "I also have the phone number of a cab company."

They laughed together as the sun sank a little lower in the sky. For a moment, Keily thought she smelled the ocean but then the moment was gone. Maybe she'd book a weekend at the coast in a month or two, just to get away for a little while.

"Excuse me, I just need to visit the little girl's room," Rosa said and walked back into the apartment.

Keily smiled. They'd been sitting there, saying nothing, and that was a good sign. When two people didn't have to fill the silence, they were comfortable around each other and that was a good thing, as far as she was concerned.

One of her phones buzzed, and from the way it sounded, she knew it was her work phone. Keily rolled her eyes and looked over at the white phone with hatred. She'd quit, find something less demanding, and leave Logan behind, if she didn't need the job so much. Rosa made it better and soon there'd be other people at the office to talk with as well. It would get better, she decided, she just had to give it time.

With a grunt of annoyance, Keily picked up the phone and stared at the message on the screen. "You've got to be kidding me."

"What now?" Rosa asked on her way back out.

"He wants me to go through 200 applications and weed out the ones that aren't good candidates."

"Um, isn't that my job?" She picked up her glass and took a sip of wine. "I think that's my job."

"It might be, but he wants me to do it. I swear…" Keily let the words trail off, feeling utterly hopeless.

"I'm sorry. Want me to help? Then it won't take so long." Rosa offered and sat up to face Keily. "We can do it tonight or I could come back tomorrow?"

Keily, usually one to brush off females she didn't know, found herself liking Rosa even more. The woman she'd thought of as competition the first time she saw her had turned out to be sweet, kind, and in need of a friend. Just like her.

"Thanks, that sounds great actually." Keily put the phone down and they discussed how they'd go about getting the work done.

"I hope he's paying you a decent salary for this," Rosa said once they had a plan worked out.

"He is, actually. He's a jerk, a really huge dick in fact, but he pays me well." Keily couldn't help the smile that danced on her lips as she thought about Logan. More precisely, his eyes, his lips, his hands, all of him, really.

He haunted her dreams, and sometimes, she fantasized about him, even at work. She couldn't understand why, he *was* a dick and he often contradicted her in front of others, on top of everything else, but something about him drew her. Maybe she was a glutton for punishment? What was that term? Masochist? Or was it sadist? Whatever, it didn't really matter, she just knew her body responded to him in ways it hadn't done since…well, that wasn't worth thinking about.

"Well, if you're willing to put up with a huge dick for a good paycheck, who am I to judge? But, really, a huge dick sounds good right about now." Rosa's eyes went wide and Keily blinked at her in pure mirth.

"Really?" Keily teased in a sing-song voice.

"That's the wine talking. I've never fantasized about Logan, I swear." She held her hand up. "He's hot, but as you said, an asshole. Assholes just aren't my type."

"I seem to attract them." Keily sipped at her drink and put the glass down. "Well, I attract them to me, not necessarily sexually."

"I'll be there for you, don't worry. When it gets to be

too much, just come to my office and we'll talk shit about him until you feel better." Rosa grinned conspiratorially and Keily relaxed even more.

Rosa could be setting her up, sure, but she doubted it. Rosa had such a warm, loving personality that she just couldn't see the woman being devious. Still, maybe she should tone it back a little. "I'll live, it's just getting used to a new boss, isn't it?"

"No, honey, he nags you more than a husband with a wife that's cut him off, and I know you know what I mean." Rosa pushed her sunglasses down a little to look over them at Keily, who had her own sunglasses on.

"I guess." Keily sighed, wishing for a moment, that Joe hadn't turned out to be such a dud. She'd invested so much of her life in him, only for him to throw it all away because he didn't get to play in the NFL.

Okay, so it had ruined her plans too, but still, she'd tried to make the best of it, make a home for him that was a sanctuary, and what had she got for her trouble? A man so drunk he either couldn't perform in the bedroom or did such a bad job of it she'd sometimes had to finish it off herself. He'd be passed out, so he hadn't known about it.

"I haven't had good sex in so long, I wouldn't know what it was, anyway. So, maybe you're right, he does kind of act like that." Keily finished with a soft laugh.

"You know, I've only been there for three days, but

I'm glad I accepted the job offer. He's been great to me, which makes it sad when he's such a dick to you, but then there's you too, you've definitely made me feel welcome."

"Good." Keily wasn't sure how to respond, she didn't want to sound desperate for a friend, but in a way, she was. "We're in early, we can be the seniors when all the freshmen come in."

"Like high school?" Rosa's head turned back to Keily. "I was such a dork in high school. All I wanted to do was get out of my parents' house and get on with my life."

"All I wanted was to marry Joe and have NFL babies." Keily said quietly.

"That was my mistake. I met Freddy at UNC, and we hit it off. But then, well, we drifted apart. He's off being some Bitcoin billionaire or something, and I'm here." Rosa blushed when she realized what she'd said and Keily smiled to let her know it wasn't taken the wrong way. "I don't mean that your place is bad, just that he lives in a mansion now, and I'm in an apartment smaller than yours."

"But would you be happy in that mansion?" Keily asked, really wondering herself now if she and Joe would have ended up living in separate wings of their mansion. "I think Joe and I would have ended up hating each other anyway. He'd have cheated all the time, I'd have been stuck home with the kids, thank goodness I used birth control while we were married."

"I think we'd have ended up the same way. Freddy's all flashy with his money now and likes the women that flock to him. I got a nice settlement from him, we didn't argue about the divorce, so that was good at least." Rosa shrugged and sipped more wine.

Hours, and another two bottles of wine later, the pair were stumbling around Keily's apartment when she noticed the time. "Rosa! It's midnight! You can't get a taxi at this time."

"Oh no!" Rosa said dramatically and put her hands to her face. "Whatever shall I do?"

They'd become more open to each other, more inclined to make each other laugh as the day wore on. "I shall save you, my lady! You take my bed and I shall occupy the couch. Worriest thee not. Wait, is worriest a word?"

"I'm not sure it is, Keily, but if it isn't it should be! And I'll take the couch." Rosa slumped down on the sofa and grinned up at Keily. "Got a blankie?"

"I has two!" Keily marched off, not caring if she was using proper English or not. She was in a playful mood and so glad Rosa had come over. "Waits, I'll find 'em."

"I only needs ones, Kei." Rosa's voice cut off on a hiccup. "Sorry, I only need one."

"No problem. I think they're in this closet." Keily

hunted until she found a white fleece blanket and brought it to her friend. Her very new friend, she thought, her only friend right now.

Not even her sister wanted to talk to her, but Violet was just jealous. Rosa was asleep by the time Keily walked back into her living room, her thoughts on her sister disappearing. "Well, here you go. I'll tuck you in."

Keily settled the soft white blanket over Rosa, noted how she'd rested her head on a pillow, just like Violet used to do when they were kids and Violet would fall asleep on the couch. Keily smiled, remembering those moments before she went off to her room.

Her feet were unsteady, even without shoes or socks on, and pain flared in her forehead as she smacked into the wall on the way to her bedroom, but that was alright. She blinked at the walls, weaving from side to side, until they turned into two walls and not six, and then managed to get to her bedroom by sliding her way down the hall.

She'd probably regret this tomorrow but fuck it. She hadn't been drunk, *really drunk*, in a long time and she needed to sleep tonight. She'd even left her phones in the kitchen. She wanted some sleep and Logan could fuck right off.

"I don't need any more of his shit tonight." She slurred to herself as she climbed into bed. "I really don't. But I could use some of his..."

She hit the pillow about that time and managed to get her comforter pulled up over her head, happy for air conditioning. It meant she could cover up, even during the summer heat. And Logan was paying the electric bill, so fuck it. Why not stay cool?

She rolled over to her right side, but that just made the room spin, so she flopped onto her back and stared up at the ceiling. That didn't help either, so she just hoped the nausea would stop or that she'd fall asleep before it got any worse. That third bottle of wine might have been one too many.

Her eyes closed and her breath evened out, but she wasn't quite asleep yet. Instead, she was fantasizing, again. Logan was such an asshole, she had to wonder if he'd be any good in bed. Would he be the same selfish jerk when it came to sex or would he take her and break her, she wondered?

She used to read these books, back before she got divorced and had time on her hands. About powerful men that came in and made their women little puddles of nothing more than want and need, willing to do anything to get even a second of the man's attention. She'd never been certain she wanted a man like that, but as the fantasy played out, she couldn't stop it.

She fell asleep with Logan on her mind. That led to a night of heated, steamy dreams that left her tossing and turning. She had no idea what he really looked like under those suave suits he wore, but her imagination made up for that. By the time she woke up in the morning, she was a mess. A thumping hangover mixed with embarrassment over the dreams meant she could barely look Rosa in the eye when she walked into the kitchen. The scent of coffee had drawn her out of the bathroom to find the solace it offered her.

"Oh, that's so good." She said carefully as she padded around in the kitchen in a bathrobe. She'd thrown her sweaty clothes off and would have taken a shower if the smell of coffee hadn't lured her out. "Coffee first, shower, maybe some toast, then work?"

"You got some aspirin?" Rosa asked with a weak smile and squinted eyes.

"I got you, girl." Keily turned and dug the pills out of a cabinet over the counter behind her. "Want some toast or anything else?"

"Toast is fine," Rosa answered and gratefully took the pills.

"That's about all I can handle."

"You might want to check your phone too, I heard it buzzing, that's what woke me up."

"Not yet. After a shower. He can be as angry as he wants to be, after I've had a shower." Keily's smile wasn't very strong either, but the coffee had already started to work. She'd have a headache most of the day, but she'd live.

Logan might fire her, or kill her, she thought as she glanced at her phone on the way to the toaster, but it didn't matter. She had a friend, and some rather sexy dreams that left her curious about the man. Very curious.

8

———————

Logan

*H*e'd given her hell all night long, mainly because he was in California and hours behind her. A rather sultry woman with dark hair and even darker eyes had come up to him at the bar of the hotel where he was staying and kept him company for a while. Her attention had kept him quiet for an hour or so. She'd offered to join him in bed when he said good night, but he'd refused.

"I've got a lot to do tomorrow or I would take you up on that offer." He put his hands around her bare biceps. Nicely muscled biceps, she kept herself fit, but he'd noted that already. He couldn't remember her name, but he knew it began with a J. "Maybe I'll see you around."

He meant it as nothing more than a brush-off. She

was beautiful, a good conversationalist, and most definitely sexy, but he only had one woman on his mind. One intolerably arrogant woman that had managed to get under his skin somehow. He downed the last dregs of his scotch, gave the woman a polite smile and a nod, and then walked out of the bar.

Keily was the most infuriating person he'd ever met, and he'd met a lot over the years. Not because she was bad at her job, or refused to meet his demands, but because he couldn't have her. And that was one thing that always drew his attention: the unattainable.

He'd worked hard to improve himself and his lot in life, but he'd learned one thing; there was always at least one factor you could not control and that was the behavior of others. Keily wasn't a pain in the ass, but she had a way of looking at him that had nearly undone him on more than one occasion.

She did her job, and did it well, despite his demands, and she never talked back, not really. She had a backbone though, and that was part of the look that she gave him. A look that said one day she'd have him under her heel, and she could be right. He'd just turned down a night of pleasure because of her.

He cursed himself for hiring her now. If he'd turned her down, thrown her application away, he could have fucked her until his dick fell off, but he hadn't done that. Oh no, he'd had to show the former cheerleader who was boss and now he was stuck. He had a strict policy about not fucking his employees. He didn't want a sexual harassment lawsuit to deal with, or anything else that came from a work relationship, on top of everything else.

He had a feeling one or two trips to his bed would get her out of his system, but he couldn't do that and there was nothing more he loved than forbidden fruit. He'd eventually gotten around to going after all the girls he shouldn't have while at university because they were forbidden to him. The cheerleaders, the rich mean girls, the ones that would have spit on him back in high school. Since then he'd had quite a few socialites, a president of a company or two, a governor of a state that would remain nameless, and quite a few more that should have been off-limits and were to the boy he'd once been. Women flocked to him now, but he only took the ones he shouldn't.

Once he'd figured out forbidden fruit was the sweetest, he'd become addicted. He'd stopped choosing the girls that actually needed and maybe deserved his attention. If they were in his league, he didn't want them. He only wanted the unattainable, those women that were too good for him. Even though he was now worth more than some small countries, he still felt like that high school kid who wanted a friend but couldn't even manage that.

Now, the woman he wanted was his employee, but remained forbidden fruit because he financed her paycheck. He walked into his hotel room, removed his suit jacket, and put it over the back of a chair. Exhaustion pulled him towards the bed, but old habits die hard. He took his pants off, placed them over the back of the chair, removed his socks and underwear, as well as his shirt, then had a shower.

He almost let thoughts of Keily fill his mind while he was in there with a slippery bar of soap. He was alone, there was nobody there to judge him or condemn him, he could get himself off, get it out of his system, but decided even that might be a step too far.

As he dried off, he thought about one option that he could take, but it would likely guarantee that he wouldn't get her in his bed. He could fire her, fuck her, and move on. The problem there was she'd hate him if he fired her. She had nowhere else to go, no car of her own, and he'd definitely catch hell if he tried to approach her with sex in mind if he took all of that away from her.

Nope, that wasn't an option then. He checked his phone and saw she hadn't responded to any of his emails or his texts. What the fuck was she doing? She was supposed to be working on a pile of applications he'd sent to her. She was either working on those or ignoring him and having a good weekend. That wasn't what he was paying her for. He set up several emails, staggered to be sent at different times, as well as text messages that would start going off at 6 am her time.

She could ignore him all she wanted to, he'd make sure she was miserable the rest of the night and the next morning. By the time he finished all that he was ready to go to sleep. It was evil of him, and it might even be petty to make her life so damned miserable, but he didn't give a fuck.

He should probably talk to someone about it but that was not something he'd ever considered doing. Not even after he'd been attacked by the football team that last time. He'd hid what had happened, he'd denied it to himself once the wounds had healed, he'd got on with life. She'd learn and do the same. He saw that same fire in her eyes that he'd had in his seven years ago. Determination could get you far. Arrogance and determination could get you further.

He put one of his favorite Led Zeppelin songs on stream and turned the last of the lights in the room off. As the well-trained fingers of Jimmy Page strummed a few introductory chords, Logan's eyes closed. It was one of his mother's favorite bands and he'd loved them from the minute he'd first heard them, apparently while he was still in the womb, according to his mother.

It wasn't exactly the kind of music that would guarantee sleep, but as the epic strains of Robert Plant's voice sang the word 'baby' over and over again, he let his thoughts go and focused solely on the song. He felt a voice calling him back home too, the same as Robert had at some point, but he knew which voice it was that called to him. It was Keily's voice and dammit, there she was again.

He got up, went to the fridge, took out a small bottle of scotch, and poured it in a glass. He raised the tumbler as if to salute the object of his current fascination and took a long drink. There was barely enough in the bottle to even call it a shot, but it went down smooth, so he pulled another bottle from the fridge and opened it. The crack of the sealed plastic broke the silence that came as his playlist ended and Robert wailed his last little bit about being lonely.

Lonely, was that it? He was lonely? No, that couldn't be it, he didn't do lonely. He could get company whenever he wanted it. He could probably go back to the bar and find that brunette still waiting there, hoping he'd come back. He had to get up early though. Wally needed him, and he was not lonely. Or so he told himself as he went back to bed.

He was just tense. He needed a little release, but the image of Keily's defiant face, small with that perfect nose that seemed to tip in just the right way to tell him to fuck off, wouldn't let him. Every time he'd looked at whatever her name was, he'd seen Keily's face. It was her voice that whispered to him that she could follow him to his room.

With a frustrated sigh, he flicked the tv on with the remote by the bed and found some documentary on wildlife in the Sahara, and left it on. That finally knocked him out, but even in his dreams, he couldn't escape her. She had the loveliest firm ass for a woman that didn't jog regularly, and her calves were just incredible. In his dreams, she wrapped those hard calves around his waist and rode him like she'd been born to do it.

At 6 am he woke up as hard as a rock, with an email from Keily making his phone blink incessantly. Seeing her name didn't ease the painful erection, but it calmed down as he opened the email to see what she'd sent. She'd managed to get the files ready then, he saw. He was impressed she'd gotten it done already. He sent back a single-word email.

Thanks.

Nothing else, just thanks. That might keep her from quitting. Salve her ego a little, he thought with a smirk as he got ready for the day. He'd ignore the last words that oozed hate at him. She'd signed her email 'ever yours' and he'd snorted about that. He could read between the lines to the 'I hope you catch syphilis and your dick falls off' that she really wanted to type.

She needed the job though and as bad as she'd been

on day one, she had improved. He could train her to be exactly what he wanted her to be without the bullshit of 'my previous employer' because Logan knew good and well she'd never earned a cent in her life. Not with the way she handled everything those first few days. At least she'd filed down those talons she came in with on day one.

Keily might be a stuck-up bitch, he thought as he went out to take the keys of his rental car from the valet, but she was smart. Which was why he'd agreed when she suggested she arrange a hotel for him. His house in California was an hour's drive from his company, he needed to be close, so she'd rented him a car and booked a hotel. Far more sensible, although he'd never tell her that. He'd just nodded and gone on with his day.

"What do you have for me, Wally?" He asked once he'd made his way to his office on the fourth floor of the brick manufacturing building that had stood through 100 years of earthquakes, floods, and a recession or two.

"We've got orders going out to Missouri that are supposed to be going to Mississippi and a fault in one of the machines that's causing defects in the tasers," Wally said promptly.

"Right, somebody in packaging messed up the postal abbreviations again, I assume, and what do we need to get the machine fixed?" He looked at the man, only a couple of years younger than him, but just as eager to learn as he'd been.

They went over those problems, as well as a few financial matters that needed his attention, and by 10 am he was on a flight back to South Carolina. He hadn't really needed to come to California but until Wally was surer about himself and his position in the company, he'd make the trips back. It kept Wally from getting too confident and making mistakes, and set both their minds at ease.

Logan could be a dick, certainly, but he cared about his employees and his company. He'd started it from nothing and he was damned if he'd let it fail due to negligence. He took a short nap on the plane and before long, he was back in the most beautiful car he'd ever owned and on his way home. First, he decided to drive by the office, just to have eyes on it.

That's what he told himself, but he knew it was a lie the minute he found himself driving by Keily's apartment. He didn't stop but he saw her hugging someone that had to be Rosa from the HR department who he'd recently hired. Keily was in a pair of short black shorts, the kind that barely covered her ass, and a loose tank top. Even in the short glimpse he got of her in the afternoon sunlight he knew she didn't have a bra on. Rosa looked a little worse for wear and he wondered just what the pair had got up to.

Countless filthy, dirty thoughts filled his mind, but he knew both women used to be married. Which could be a good reason to explore, he thought as he pulled back out onto the road and hoped neither of the women had spotted him as he drove by. The windows were tinted, so they wouldn't have seen his face at least.

He felt like an idiot as he drove away, certain that they'd spotted him now. He didn't want to start rumors and he'd never admit to Keily that he'd driven by but if she asked, he'd have a hard time thinking up a reason as to why he might have been near her place. Checking to make sure she'd settled in, he decided. If he bothered to admit the truth to her.

He headed to his own place, ordered some takeout, and spent the rest of the evening preparing for the next day. He'd already emailed Keily to tell her to set up appointments for the next batch of manager positions he'd interview for, then told her to send the rest to Rosa. He wanted to see if she'd say anything about Rosa.

"You want Rosa to hire the factory staff? I'll let her know. Hope your weekend was nice." She sent back promptly. Not a hint of a word about Rosa or that she'd just left Keily's apartment. Just a quick, concise response.

Hmm. Now, what did that mean? She didn't want him to know she'd made friends with the other woman? The messy style of both women's hair could be described as sex-hair, that messy mane that a good session could produce. But it could also just be a long day of work, or a trek out to hike. Maybe they'd been exercising or something. Rosa was a physically fit woman, that could be it.

Surely his conquest hadn't suddenly decided to be a lesbian, had she? Not before he got his hands on her. But he couldn't get his hands on her, he reminded himself. Best to just forget about her in that way and torture the fuck out of her until she quit. With a deep breath, Logan decided that's exactly what he'd do. But he'd also try to figure out if she had some kind of relationship with Rosa too. Just out of curiosity. It wasn't jealousy at all.

9

Keily

The swish of the elevator doors was now a familiar sound as Keily walked towards the windows in the office the next morning, her right hand out to grab the wand that would pull the blinds back. She paused and looked out at the buildings across the street as sunlight started to glint from windows and the metal of 50-year-old signs that had long ago lost their paint. Once upon a time, the street had been lively with workers bustling back and forth, but now, it was a quiet place, almost deserted.

The town had been on its deathbed for a long time, but now? Well, she thought as she turned back to face the office and go to her desk, now maybe Logan had given some people hope. After the weekend she'd had, all she'd really wanted to do was send him a rudely worded email and stay home, but she wouldn't have a home without him.

It wasn't fair, but what could you do? With a sigh of resignation, she put down the travel mug of coffee she'd brought from home and deposited her handbag into one of the deep drawers of her desk. Before she closed the drawer, she took out both her phones and placed them at the edge of her desk.

Oddly enough, there'd been no messages or emails from Logan when she got up, he'd been quiet all morning too. It was habit to get up early now and check all her messages and emails while she waited on her coffeemaker to gurgle its last drops, but this morning? Nothing.

For a moment, she wondered if he was ill, or if he'd been in an accident, but then she heard the elevator as it stopped on her floor and looked up. "Good morning, Logan?"

She didn't mean to turn it into a question but that's what happened.

He glared at her for a quiet moment, then his face cleared, and she almost smiled at him. Almost.

"So it is. I'll be in my office." He made a sound that might have been a grunt as he walked by her desk and into his office. He closed the door as he went into the room and this time it was Keily that frowned.

What was wrong with him?

She put her elbows on her desk and her head in her hands as she thought about him. He wore a blue silk suit with a slight sheen to it, impeccable in all ways, as always, with his hair neatly combed and his skin a healthy color, so what was wrong with him? Had the trip not gone well?

Maybe that was it.

She waited for instructions of some kind, but after ten minutes, when he didn't come out of his office, she decided to get up and find something to do. Last Friday they'd sent out emails inviting people for job interviews and they'd come streaming in within a couple of hours.

He played on her mind as she went through the motions, putting together packets for the interviews later. Some would be hired, some wouldn't be, but the ones that were hired needed to have packets ready, with contracts, papers to sign, and forms to fill out. She went through the files the PA out in California had sent along to her and printed off each one as a master copy.

She laughed softly as she found herself humming while she printed copies of each packet and placed them in plain white file folders. For once, she was happy. Her hangover was gone, she had a good job, even if her boss was a jerk, and she was making friends with a woman that was kind and good company.

Not that long ago, she'd been happy scamming drinks out of businessmen in suits, on their way to some important meeting or winding down a little before they went home to their wives and families. She'd had no goals in mind, resented her sister, and had no reason to smile at all.

Now she had a job, her very own home, both for the first time in her life, and she felt real pride, something she hadn't felt in years. Not since her cheerleading days when she pulled off a complicated move that the other girls couldn't. The sensation of warmth that swelled in her chest expanded when she saw her bank balance increase when her pay was deposited into her account. Now it was Monday, and any minute she expected he'd come out of the office where he was hiding and ruin her day.

She took a deep breath and told herself today would be different, she could feel it. He'd come in late, grumped at her, then hidden himself away. Something was up, but as long as it meant she had a quiet day for once, she didn't care. Maybe she'd even get to go home in time to use the pool at the apartment that she still hadn't even gone out to look at. Normally, she got home late, too tired, irritated, and hungry to even look in the direction of the pool. By the time she'd showered, had dinner, and answered Logan's seemingly never-ending stream of emails and text messages she forgot the pool even existed.

Her thoughts turned back to the files she was copying when the machine came to a sudden stop and beeped at her. She'd taken the time to figure out how to change the ink cartridges, put in the paper, and how to use the different functions of the thing when Logan went out for lunch on day one. He'd wanted her to copy some files and she had no idea how to do it, so she'd taken the initiative and looked for videos online. Once she watched those it had been no problem.

She could go down to the supply room for the entire office, but she'd filled a small closet with the supplies they used the most on this floor. It was down the hall by the private bathrooms. She took a right by the reception area, opened the door there, and headed down to the closet.

The ink cartridges were way in the back of the deep closet, behind stacks of paper she'd lugged up and stacked on the shelves. Why did she put them in the very back? she wondered now and pulled some of the stacks of paper out to reach further in back. Her fingers brushed against a box and she snatched at it and pulled it out.

"Ah-ha!" She said with a note of pride and moved to turn away from the closet but bumped into something.

That something was a solid, steely wall of man and that man was Logan.

"Oh, sorry." Her head sank down, and she stared at the ink cartridge with a deep frown. It wasn't even the right one, she needed the black ink, not the color ink!

"It's alright. Got the wrong one, did you?" He asked with a hint of a smirk on his lips. "Allow me."

He was so close she could feel him pressing her into the door, but she didn't try to step away. Her brain kept telling her feet to move but they wouldn't budge. His arm brushed against her bustline and she felt a small thrill that went all the way down to her stomach and became a bloom of something deeper than thrill.

She could smell the refreshing scent of his cologne, something that smelled cool instead of warm, that made her want to draw nearer to him. But she couldn't do that without pressing up against him on purpose and, so far, this was all accidental. She didn't want him to know she was attracted to him, hell, she didn't actually want to admit to herself that she was attracted to him.

When she first started working for him, she'd had plans of seducing him, maybe even having a long affair, until she got on her feet again. But after weeks of his asshole behavior, she'd abandoned that idea.

"This the one you want?" He pulled back suddenly, and his face was just a kiss away from hers.

Awareness crackled to life within Keily and she

wanted to grasp at his shoulders, pull him closer, kiss him until they were both too caught up in each other to know where they were. Her eyes fell to his lips while her own relaxed and drew closer to his. Time stood still as her eyes began to close, and she felt his hand on her hip. He was about to kiss her, and she couldn't, wouldn't move away.

"Well, ahem, that's that then." He pulled away, moved towards the bathrooms. "I need those packets so if you can stop playing around in the closet, I'd appreciate it. I'm paying you to work, not goof off."

"I wasn't…" she started to answer him, but stopped when he turned back to her, his face a hairsbreadth from rage.

"What's that now?" He marched back, his face growing darker, until she pressed back into the door again, her face tilted up to look into his eyes. "I don't need your excuses, Keily. You're terrible at this job, and we both know it, but I keep you on because where else would you go? I could hire ten other people to do your job right now, and each one would be better at it than you are. So, please, don't go getting ideas about talking back to me, you understand?"

His hand was back on her hip and with each word he spoke his face drew infinitesimally closer to hers. Tears filled her eyes at his cruel words, but her body betrayed her. It wanted him, yearned to feel more of his touch, and she couldn't look away from those stormy brown eyes that held her in thrall.

"Keily?" His finger came up, ran along her jawline until her head tilted even further up. "Do you understand me? You're here because I *pity* you."

He said the words so softly as if they were a caress equal to the light touch of his finger on her jawline, but they felt like the lash of a whip across her spine. Her face pulled away, anger flashed in her eyes, and he smiled down at her, his eyes full of mirthful amusement.

"Now, go on and be a good girl and do your job." He patted her cheek before he walked away, a cocky swagger followed by a soft chuckle his parting shot.

Fucking asshole.

She wanted to turn around, to tell him where he could fuck off to, or just walk out of the building and not come back to work for him, but she pulled it back. She thought of what would happen when she told Violet that she'd quit her job and would have to move back in, and how Violet would laugh, maybe even refuse. Of how Violet would mock her and tell her what a failure she was, deservedly so apparently. She bit down on her tongue to keep her mouth closed.

She'd go and talk to Rosa later maybe, get her help in calming down. For now, she went to the printer, changed the cartridge, and printed off the packets with her brain on autopilot. Do not think about it, do not think about him, do not think about how he'd cut her to the very bone with his words.

A tear slid from her eye and rolled down her cheek. She swiped it away, but another quickly followed, dripped from her eye and down to the printer. She stared at the clear liquid that now made a single spot on the plastic shine and wondered if this was how her life would be from now on? Had she agreed to work for the devil in return for a home and a car? For the luxuries she'd missed after her divorce?

Damn, she wasn't even getting fucked, at least then it might be worth it. She laughed silently at herself. Did she really want to fuck a man that obviously hated her? But why did he hate her so much? She put the papers in order, tucked them into folders, then put them on his desk since he'd left the office to take care of something down in the factory.

She looked around his office. It was neat, tidy, everything in place, the proper kind of office a very rich man should have. It revealed nothing about him, though. There were no degrees or certificates on the walls, only whiteboards and a metal sheet that he used magnets to pin papers to. There were usually plans for the factory on that sheet, prototype images, things like that. It was empty today and the whiteboard was clean. He had strangers coming in soon for interviews.

That was actually Rosa's job, but he'd decided to be

hands-on for the first set of employees. Rosa had told her the plan was for him to hire, her to fire, if need be. She'd walk the new people through their jobs, assign them to department managers, and go over their benefits with them. Later, she'd hire replacements and go through evaluations with them.

For a moment, Keily envied Rosa her job; she didn't have to deal with Logan so often. Keily took one final glance around the office and went back to her desk. She'd cleaned the entire space, even though the place was cleaned every evening. She'd printed off the packets and there was nothing else for her to do. She stared at her computer, then at her phone. He'd pop up any minute now with a demand, some order that she'd have to address immediately, but nothing happened.

He left her alone, which was odd. Something must be wrong with him, but what? A few minutes before the lunch hour, with her pride still stinging, Keily waited for some kind of direction from him. Her phone buzzed and she looked down to see it was Rosa.

"Want to meet down at the Old Barrel for lunch?" The text message read.

"Yes, please, meet you downstairs in five?" She typed back and grabbed her bag from the drawer. She left a note on Logan's door since he was still out, and walked to the elevator.

The man was infuriating, had taken a chunk out of

her pride and would probably continue to do so, but she'd go down, have lunch with Rosa, and come back feeling better about it all. That, or she'd find a new job and quit this one. Hot or not, Logan had hurt her deeply and she wasn't sure she could deal with that. He pitied her and that nearly broke her. Even if she wouldn't admit it to anyone, ever.

10

Logan

Keily was a savvy woman. He'd come to realize that over the last few weeks, ever since that moment they'd almost kissed. At one time in his life, he'd have given anything to get a kiss from a woman like Keily, yet he'd stopped himself that day. He was angry with himself for letting his control slip, he'd taken it out on her but she was a trooper.

Savvy as he'd thought a moment ago, he reminded himself. Most women would have quit after that encounter. He'd deliberately picked his words and his actions. He'd been careful to provoke outrage, maybe even tears. Instead, she'd steeled her backbone, met his every glance, and didn't back down. Smart, sexy, brave. She was all of those things as well.

She was in a new outfit today, a black pencil skirt with a floral blouse that suited the cold temperature he kept the office at. He preferred cooler temperatures, and the light sweater she wore over her blouse, a pale blue shade that highlighted the almost clear quality of her eyes, attested to how much she didn't like the cold.

He'd noted that with each new paycheck she added to her wardrobe, one piece or another that would still have that new clothing smell when she walked in wearing it. A skirt, a top, new shoes. He especially liked the black stilettos she'd invested in. They did incredible things for her calves and he liked to watch her walk around the office in them.

He closed the email he'd received a few moments ago and leaned over a little to watch as she walked around the office. Keily was not who she said she was, not at all, but he loved looking at those legs of hers.

"Keily?" He called out as she neared his open door and smiled when she leaned in with an arched eyebrow.

"Yes, Logan?" Her curious eyes took him in without a hint of anything to give away her thoughts. She'd become cold to him, unflinching and distant, but she did her job well, now that she'd caught on to what was necessary. He'd taken it easy on her for the last couple of weeks, even stopped organizing emails to go out in the middle of the night.

Since that almost-kiss four weeks ago, it just seemed

petty. Keily had proven herself capable of learning fast, thinking quickly on her feet, and getting the job done.

An idea had occurred to him, and he knew it was probably a bad idea, but couldn't stop himself now that he'd called her in.

"There's a company dinner tonight, I need you to accompany me." He sat at his desk and looked up at her with guileless brown eyes. He didn't give away the slightest hint that anything was wrong or that he'd just had it confirmed that she didn't have a degree of any kind.

"Of course, where and what time?" She didn't even blink those incredible gray eyes or question him; she just did as she was told. That thrilled him on a deeper, private level that he didn't want to admit to. At least, not with her in the doorway.

He told her the location and time and she nodded quietly, "I'll be there."

"Thank you, you can get back to work now."

He shooed her out, but he doubted she noticed, she'd already turned around to walk out of the office.

"Jennifer?" He heard her say from her desk a few minutes later. "Where are those reports for last night's production?"

A pause and Logan assumed she was listening to Jennifer, the supervisor for the third shift at the factory. The woman had probably been asleep but Keily didn't seem to care. She took her cues from Logan; if you needed information, you got it, one way or another.

"No, I don't really care that you'd just fallen asleep, Jennifer. Logan needs those numbers so email them to me if nothing else." He heard Keily give a deep sigh and then the sound of the phone being placed back in the cradle.

She could be bossy with other employees, but she needed to be. She could be nicer to them, sure, but she wanted to make sure Logan had everything he needed every day. It didn't matter what the excuse was, Logan came first.

What would it be like to come first in her world if they were in a relationship? Would she be as devoted, as doggedly ferocious about meeting her partner's needs?

"Hi, Keily, I need to see Logan, please." He heard from the outer office after a ding from the elevator.

"No, he's not to be disturbed right now." She knew that because it was one pm and normally he'd be on the phone with the California office and Wally.

Things had finally started to smooth out, however, and there were no problems that needed to be sorted out today, so he'd put off the call for a while. He listened to Keily instead. She was a bossy little thing, that was for sure.

"You can come back later if you want to see him."

Her tone was crisp, not to be trifled with, and that made Logan smile.

"But, Keily, I really need to talk to Logan about my parking space. It's too far from the building." The male voice whined and Logan cringed at the tone. That wouldn't bring Keily to disturb his call at all even if the man seemed to think it would.

"Then come back in two hours. It's impossible, you can't see him right now." Her voice grew harder, sterner, as she continued and he would bet a thousand dollars that her eyes were like two gray shards of ice right now.

"Fine, but I'm telling him you wouldn't let me in." The male voice, a guy named Matt who was on his way to being fired for lack of performance, amongst other things, threatened.

Logan's lips quirked into a smile; he knew what was coming next.

"Good, you do that, Matt. He'll probably give me a raise for keeping you out of his office over something so trivial, now go back to work, if you can find your office."

He'd hired Matt as a third shift supervisor because he had experience, but the man seemed to have a drug problem. Some shifts he was up, busy as a bee, high as a kite perhaps, while others he was strung out, couldn't focus, and messed up far too many of his duties.

Keily was perfect at her job now and they made a good team, Logan realized a while ago. Once she'd found her backbone again, that is. He wondered if he'd completely crushed it with his harshness that day when he almost kissed her all those weeks ago, but she'd finally started to blossom.

People might not like her, besides Rosa that is, but she did her job excellently and that was what he needed, not someone that everyone liked. If they all liked her, they'd walk all over her, but her pushiness, her no-nonsense attitude got the job done, in their office and in the contacts she made with other companies. Especially suppliers, who feared getting a call from her, he was certain of it. Which was part of the reason he hadn't fired her right away when he got the email. She was too damned good at doing her job.

Two bullies in a pod, was that it, he wondered? They were both bent on being in charge, although she did defer to him. Was he the bully now?

If he was, he didn't care, it made her job performance improve and he wouldn't regret that. But perhaps he could reward her a little, even if she had lied about her degree. He could show her that he wasn't all bad. Dinner seemed like a good plan, especially a public one. If they were in public, he wouldn't be so tempted to touch her, to pull her close and feel that luscious body of hers against his.

Nope, stop that right now. He picked up his phone to

call the California office and stopped thinking about Keily.

When he was finished with the other office, he left the building and headed out to have the oil changed in his car. It was a new car and he was definitely going to take care of it. He could have someone do the job for him, but he liked the task and could do with some time out of the office anyway.

"I'll be out for the rest of the day, Keily, take messages and forward them to me if you need to."

"Certainly." She answered promptly, with a dark blonde brow lifted as if she'd taken offense that he imagined she might not.

He liked keeping her on her toes like that. Keeping her in her place, even.

It was nice to know that the former head cheerleader had fallen so low she was now his personal assistant. Head cheerleaders were the bane of his existence back in high school and, well, Keily still had that air about her, that superiority, an air of self-importance that wasn't earned at all, not when it came to the real world.

He headed to a local garage, one he remembered from back in the day, not sure if it was still open or not. He was surprised to find it still there, out in the sticks a little on the outskirts of town, but still there. Logan couldn't remember the man's name but didn't let it bother him.

"Hi there, old-timer, I need the oil changed, can you handle it?" He asked the old man who looked at him with squinted eyes and a little bit of a sneer. Logan suspected the squint was from a case of near-sightedness that required glasses, but the old man probably wouldn't wear them.

"I reckon, if I can get the filter, that is. Might take a few hours. You got anywhere to be?"

"No, not really."

The bald man, as wrinkled and brown as a black walnut walked closer to Logan. "Don't I know you?"

"Maybe, I'm from here, but it's been a while. Name's Logan Sinclair."

"Right, don't know any Sinclairs. Let me get on the phone now, son, find that filter. If you get bored, I got an old truck in the back, you can hop in and head back into town if you want."

"You'd trust me like that?" Logan asked, surprised but with a smile on his face.

"Sure, I've got this baby all to myself if you don't bring my heap of junk back." The old man cackled, and Logan laughed with him.

"I guess you're right, Eddie." Logan had finally remembered the man's name and they shook hands before Eddie handed over the keys.

Logan went out to the back of the old garage, built in the 1970s and typical of that era, with a storefront to one side and two garage doors for cars on the other. A 1950s Ford truck of some kind, blue in patches, gray and rust-colored in others, sat in the back. Logan frowned at the vehicle but decided he'd fill the tank up and take a ride around town, see what other memories he could dredge up about the place.

There were a few good memories to find. The swimming hole that was about a mile from where his parents had lived, a hot place to walk to in the summer, but nice once you got there. Logan found a house on the hill above the pond with a fence around it now, with a sign reading 'no entry to the public'. He wondered if kids still snuck in at night to get a little relief from the muggy South Carolina nights. If they were brave enough to fend off the mosquitos that is.

He went back down the road, found a gas station, put some gas in the tank, and headed out to another spot, a small sheltered park that was part of a historical plantation museum. He wasn't much for revisiting the past, but he liked the quiet peace of shaded trees with a bench in the middle of the copse to be found there. He'd spent many a day there, winter and summer, doing homework while tourists gawked at the plantation not far away. They all dreamed about Scarlett O'Hara and Rhett Butler, but Logan knew the history of the place.

The owners were brutal, had kept slaves, and every generation seemed to get worse until there was only one old man left, and he'd left the plantation to the state to be used as a museum. A fitting end, Logan thought. Those that earned their fame, their money, their privilege off the back of others didn't deserve to be remembered, to have continued success. He might be a dick to Keily, but the rest of his staff were well-paid, as was she, with generous benefits packages. He would never allow himself to be compared to that slave-owning family of the past or some of the larger corporations that now profited from the desperate and needy.

He wouldn't stoop that low, because he'd been one of those deprived people a very long time ago, and he knew what it was like. He'd come a long way from those days, but he'd never forget being called poor white trash, and knowing that's exactly what he was. Maybe not anymore, but he had been, and he wouldn't look down on anyone but those that thought they were better than others. He'd make sure he'd take those people down a peg or two. As he'd done with Keily and would continue to do.

11

Keily

A dinner with Logan. Keily frowned as she stared off into space, wondering what to wear. She'd thought about it all afternoon, and finally she decided to buy something new on her way home. She pulled into the parking lot of a boutique on Main Street and turned the car off. There was something perfect in the window of the shop and she decided she'd have it if it wasn't too expensive.

It was black silk, a halter-style dress, with a ribbon under the bust. The dress flared out from that ribbon down to just around her knees. It wasn't a casual dress by any means but not too showy for a dinner at Marisco's with Logan. Well, with Logan and whoever else was coming. Logan had mentioned it was a company dinner but hadn't said if they were meeting clients or someone else.

As she took off the dress in her size that the saleswoman brought to her and put her clothes back on, she wondered if it was really a company dinner or not. It hadn't been on his schedule so perhaps this was just a ploy to get her out of the office and to have dinner with him?

"I'll take it." She told the saleswoman with a smile and waited as she folded the dress up and scanned the price tag.

"It suits you very much." The woman said with a polite smile and Keily nodded her thanks before she handed over her debit card.

Once she was home, she showered, dried her hair, and put on fresh makeup. Her fingers shook with nervousness that only increased as each minute passed. She wasn't sure why she was so nervous she just knew she was. Well, it wasn't really that hard to figure out, not really, it was Logan.

If this was some kind of ploy, then she could be about to walk into a trap. Since that day by the closet, Logan had become nicer to her. Sure, he'd nearly broken her with his cruel words, but he'd calmed down since that moment. He didn't harass her nearly as much as he'd once done, but there was still steel in his eyes when he looked at her.

Did he want her? she wondered and stared into the mirror above the bathroom sink. He could have his pick of women, why would he want a former cheerleader that was now his PA? Another notch in his belt, perhaps?

And why was she even considering an affair now? She'd almost quit, the man was so insufferable, but now she was nearly giggling over the thought of sleeping with him. It was all stupid, she knew that, but despite his cruelty, she couldn't help but think about the way he stared at her that day by the closet.

Heat had filled his eyes, hunger too, and she'd known what real desire looked like. Sure, Joe had wanted her, but he'd had her so easily that she'd never seen him truly hungry for her. Logan, on the other hand, hadn't, and it had been over a month since he'd almost kissed her.

For a moment Keily felt almost…virginal. She wasn't a temptress, had no real idea about how to be a seductress either. She'd batted her eyelashes at her ex a lifetime ago and that had been all there was to it. Logan, however, was a man, one used to adult games.

With a sigh, she slipped her shoes on and walked out of the apartment, bag in hand. No matter what game Logan was playing, she was certain she could win. She lifted her chin, strode to the car with confidence, and was on her way with a smile on her face.

Rosa called almost the instant she was out of the

parking lot and Keily hit the button to accept the call through her car's Bluetooth system.

"Hey, you ready for this dinner with the beast?" Rosa asked and Keily chuckled softly over the name they'd started to call him.

"Not really, but I'm almost there."

"Well, good luck. You're beautiful and no matter who's there, you'll outshine them all." Rosa always said the nicest things to her and now was no different.

"Thanks, but you'd outshine me if you were there," Keily replied instantly and meant it.

"I doubt that," Rosa answered and brushed it all away with a laugh. "Anyway, I know you won't need it, but good luck again. Let me know how it goes."

"I will." Keily couldn't help the real smile that spread over her face at her friend's words. It was nice to have someone that believed in you. "And thanks, Rosa."

"Talk to you later, Kei, have fun." Rosa hung up before Keily could answer, but Keily didn't mind. She was almost at the restaurant anyway.

A stoplight added two minutes to her drive-time, but it gave her a chance to go over her plan for the night. It would be monumentally stupid to get involved with her boss, but she knew she wouldn't turn him down if he made any kind of overture to her. It was so cliché, the boss and the secretary, but he was gorgeous, and she hadn't been with a man since well before she divorced Joe.

If nothing else, she'd get to flirt with whoever else was at the restaurant. Maybe there'd be some other guy there, one that would welcome her attention. She didn't want a new husband, she'd only just found out what independence was like, but she wouldn't turn down some fun with the right man.

She pulled into the parking lot of the most expensive restaurant in King's Hill and parked the car close to the front door. Her heels were three-inch stilettos and she could walk in them, but her legs would start to ache if she had to walk too far. She only wore them on special occasions, mainly when she knew she wouldn't have to stand up for long.

One last check of her makeup and she was on her way into the restaurant. She walked in and gave Logan's name to the woman that greeted her. She licked her lips nervously and tucked a lock of hair behind her ear as she made her way to the table where Logan sat alone.

He quickly stood up to greet her with a smile on his face and she remembered all those times she'd caught him looking at her. He was interested in her, but she was used to that. Men often looked at her with sexual interest and she'd thrived on it throughout her life. What had been missing with all the others was that hungry look she'd only ever seen on him.

It was there as she walked up to him, but now that he'd got a hold on his emotions it was gone. She looked up at him, curious as to what his reaction would be.

"You look lovely, Keily. Thanks for coming. Won't you sit down?" He showed her to the place beside his own on the booth seat and she slid into the spot.

It was a long, white leather booth, designed to hold at least six people, with another booth across from it in the romantically lit room. The long table was covered in a maroon tablecloth with real candles along the length. Each tea candle was snuggled into a white-frosted holder that reflected the light softly, without too much illumination.

"Thank you." She answered as she settled into the position and looked around. "Am I early?"

His sheepish grin told her all she needed to know as he re-took his seat. "It seems I got the dates wrong."

He was dressed in a pair of black slacks with a tight black t-shirt that she knew must have cost hundreds of dollars by the quality alone. It wasn't any ordinary t-shirt, that was for sure. She looked up at his face after she examined his body and smirked just a little. She still had it then.

"I did wonder, your calendar was empty." She said, knowing he'd get her point. She'd known all along this was a ruse to get her out, away from the office.

Maybe it wasn't the best idea to play this game. She'd

learned to be standoffish with him, impersonal and cold even, but the minute she'd left work earlier it was like a switch had flipped in her brain and she'd gone from efficient PA to budding seductress. Even now she could almost feel the way her eyes sparkled up at him.

His eyes narrowed but he didn't reply other than to give a slight tilt of his head.

"May I get you something to drink?" A blond-haired waiter asked and Keily looked up at him, away from the man who might be too dangerous for her own good.

"A glass of red wine, please." She answered instantly and then looked back at Logan, curiosity clear in the way she examined his features.

She was willing to find out if he was as dangerous as her brain now warned he was. It surprised her, but she missed Alice and Violet, the nights of a house filled with noise and constant companionship. She came home to a quiet, empty apartment now. And since Logan had stopped making so many demands on her time, she'd come to notice just how quiet the place really was. He might only be offering companionship for the night, but she hoped he was offering more.

Even one night away from that empty apartment would be nice, though.

She'd come out tonight wondering, willing sex to be on the menu. Now that she was here and he was only inches away from her, she was still willing, but logic was creeping in like a trickle of ice water that threatened to become a flood. Could she really handle a single night with a man as intense as Logan?

"I appreciate that you came out, really. I didn't mean to waste your time." His face turned to her and she sat back in the booth.

Suddenly, he was too near, too real, and she wondered if she'd been too confident, too convinced of her ability to handle Logan. Maybe he was the one doing the handling and she was just along for the ride, too naïve to know when she was in over her head?

"You're welcome, Logan." She responded quietly, and looked down at the table, desperate to look away from the promises hidden behind his gaze.

You can do this, she reminded herself, not completely sure that was the truth.

He tilted his head and she looked back at him, wondering what he was about to say next. Something about the way his lips pursed, the way his eyebrows pulled together was oddly familiar and she frowned.

For some reason, she knew that look. Déjà vu made goosebumps pop up over her skin and she looked at him more closely. She'd known him for a few weeks now, spent many hours with him since he'd hired her and she'd never felt it, but now, looking at him closely, she knew that she'd met him somewhere before. Where that might have been, she had no idea and wondered if she was just imagining it.

"What do you want to eat?" He asked, and her concentration was broken.

It was ridiculous, thinking she knew him from somewhere. She'd never met him until she walked into his office that day. He'd have said they knew each other if they did, wouldn't he?

12

Logan

*L*ogan had time to think about the information he'd received that morning as the day wore on and he was in knots about what to do about it. Normally, if he found out one of his employees lied about their degree, he'd have them fired immediately. What to do about little Ms. Keily though? He was still pondering what he should do when she showed up in a dress designed to slay even the most staunchly celibate of men. He wasn't even slightly inclined to celibacy and had next to no defense against the dress or the sultry look in her eyes.

This dinner was just supposed to be a way to show he wasn't a complete asshole and could be nice to her, but that dress. Damn, why did she have to be so fucking beautiful?

He was in trouble, and he knew it.

"Another glass of wine?" He asked as she tilted the glass to her lips.

Perfectly red lips, even without lipstick. Lips made for...

"No, a glass of water please." She smiled as she spoke, her eyes locked on his.

"Of course." He replied smoothly, as if his brain wasn't melting down and his pants weren't about to spontaneously combust from the heat pulsing through his veins.

He was a master of hiding his thoughts, his emotions, he reminded himself. He just had to remember why he was supposed to do any of that. That was hard to do when Keily was all things tempting and dangerous.

It was one thing when she swept into his office with her hair in a tight bun and wisps of makeup on, wearing those frumpy cardigans to chase off the cold in his office. It was another thing entirely when she'd made an effort and had on those black heels that he loved so very much on her.

The heels that he could picture from behind because he'd watched her walking away in them so many times.

"So, what are we going to do if this is a business

dinner, Logan? Talk about my filing techniques?" Her tone was teasing, coaxing him into a playful mood.

He shouldn't have done this, he decided. He might be prepared to take on female governors and company CEOs, but Keily was something else entirely. She was a part of his past, one he'd tried to forget, but couldn't because so many people owed him from those days. Including her.

"Well, ahem, I guess we can just eat, Keily." He swallowed around the knot in his throat and went on. "You've worked hard over the last few weeks, your skills have improved, and well, you deserve a night off. For a little while."

"Oh. Thanks, Logan." She smiled and her brows knitted together in a way that Logan thought was…cute.

"It's true." He shifted around in his seat, nervous for the first time in years. "Excuse me, please."

"Of course." She said as he got out of his seat and walked quickly to the bathroom. He didn't need to go, he just needed to get his mind under control again. He smoothed his hair down, washed his hands, took a couple of deep breaths, and headed back out to the table.

He slid into the booth and looked over at her and his thoughts scattered immediately. Damn. Even hurriedly putting her phone away was sexy when Keily did it. He smiled to cover the awkward moment before he spoke. "Anyway, what are you going to have?"

"Pardon?" She asked, thrown off by the unexpected question.

"For dinner? What do you want?" He pointed at the menu she hadn't touched yet with a smile meant to disarm.

Don't think about how soft her lips look or how her cleavage swells over her dress with every breath she takes, just focus on...dinner.

"Oh, right, let me look."

His thoughts turned back to the things he'd found out earlier that day. She'd never been to a university, although she had done a lot of schoolwork for her ex. Her ex had been a football player on a scholarship, with no real academic goals. From what Logan had learned from his private detective, she'd been the one that did all the schoolwork, while Joe had been busy playing on the field.

She also had no former employer. There was no work history for her, anywhere, and the employer she'd listed had apparently never existed. Which meant she'd lied about everything on her resume and during the interview. He should have looked it all up before now, but he'd put it off. He'd been intrigued by her from the start, he'd had a plan when he asked her in for an interview, but over the last few weeks, as he'd come to know her even superficially, he'd learned to have some respect for her.

She was tenacious, willing to learn, and willing to do whatever it took to make sure his demands were met. She'd gone from being afraid to make a mistake, to owning up to them and fixing them without being told. But now, he had to fire her. She'd lied, what else could he do?

She's a really great PA, though, he reminded himself as the waiter came back with a glass of water and to take their order. Logan ordered whatever steak they had without much thought to what he'd eat, and he didn't hear what she ordered. He was too caught up in his own thoughts about what he'd learned.

"How are you tonight, Logan?" She asked once the waiter left.

He blinked at her, surprised that she'd spoken up.

His thoughts whirled around in his head so much it was difficult to focus on one thing.

"I'm fine, Keily. Tell me about your ex." He changed the subject, eager to not talk about himself.

"About Joe? What do you want to know?" Her smile was brittle, and he knew she didn't want to talk about Joe at all.

"Why did you divorce him?" He was on that train now so he might as well ride it, he decided.

"Well, there was the fact that he was an alcoholic. He blew his knee out in college and the NFL team that was about to draft him dropped him instead. That started it,

I guess. He had to fall back on the communications degree he, excuse me..." She took a drink of her water as if to swallow down something bitter she didn't want to taste, and continued, "earned."

She paused, took a deep breath, and then carried on. "He continued to drink, but I thought he had it under control. Until he got fired from the station he worked for, that is. He used to do the local news, but that all ended badly and it was impossible to stand by and watch him drink himself to death, so I divorced him."

A shrug of her pretty shoulders punctuated her final statement and he nodded. He had to wonder if Joe's drinking was all that had ended their marriage. Logan had read about the violence so many former sports players brought to those around them even years after leaving the respective games. He'd seen images splashed on screens of men with violent rage on their faces and in their hands and wondered if Joe had ever laid a finger on her.

He'd kill the guy if he had.

But that meant Keily would have to tell him those things had happened, and that would mean a lot more talks than he planned to have with her. He still couldn't decide whether to fire her or not, having that kind of conversation with her was definitely not going to take place any time soon.

"Right." Logan nodded and tried to think of something else to say.

"What about you? Have you ever been married?"

"No, not even close." He shook his head to punctuate the statement. "You grew up here, you said?"

Deflect questions, that was the best thing to do when you didn't want to talk about yourself.

"Yeah, I was born in the local hospital. Mom and Dad brought me home and I've lived here ever since. They moved to Florida a few months ago, but the house is still there." She paused, a smile on her face.

"Was it a nice childhood?" It was just something to keep her talking, he didn't really need to ask. Women like her always had nice childhoods.

"Yeah, it was. I was a cheerleader, the prom queen, all that good stuff." She waved her hand a little on the table as if to dismiss it but from the way she smiled and the pride in her eyes, he knew she was proud of her past. Normally, that wouldn't be a bad thing.

"And Joe? How did you meet him?"

She paused, frowned, and he knew she was wondering why he was so curious about Joe. He wasn't about to give her an answer though.

She shrugged again and smiled. "We met in school when we were kids. Dated all through high school, got married after graduation, then went off to, uh, well we went to the same university."

He'd noticed how she stumbled there and knew she still wasn't used to the lie she'd told him. For now, she was too good an employee to let go so he'd keep her on. For now.

"Right, your university days. You were a cheerleader there too?"

She nodded but looked away. "Where's that waiter, I could use some more water."

"I'll see if I can get him over here."

Logan caught the waiter's eye and held up Keily's empty water glass.

Their food arrived soon after and they both went quiet as they ate. Logan had no idea if the steak was good or not because he couldn't stop watching Keily. She had impeccable table manners no doubt taught to her by the same mother that had taken her to all of those beauty pageants. The way she ate delicately and with care was somehow seductive, though. As if every turn of her wrist or push of a finger was designed to draw the eye of every man in the room.

By the time she put her fork and knife down he was ready to drag her under the table, and that was a whole new experience for him. He agreed to a slice of chocolate pie just to get the waiter to go away once their empty plates were removed. Keily picked up the bottle of red wine he'd ordered earlier with a quirked eyebrow.

"May I?" She asked softly and he nodded mutely.

Keily was a fascinating woman. She was everything you'd expect, but there was far more to her than he thought people had ever given her credit for. He admired that, even if he didn't want to admit it.

"What are your plans for the rest of the evening, Keily?" His voice was little more than a murmur, but she heard him.

Her head swiveled to face him, and her eyes narrowed.

"Well, my sister will either be at home with her baby or at work, my parents live several hours away, and I don't have a lot of friends." That last part wasn't said with self-pity, it was just stated as a fact. "I don't have many plans most of the time, actually."

"I see. So, you could do some work for me this evening?" He felt bad about the way her eyes lost their sparkle and the way her lips pursed, but he had to get this back on track.

This was just a thank you dinner, not a seduction dinner, after all. He knew he could have both, have her, but it was such a bad idea. A really, really bad idea.

She put her elbow on the table, put her cheek in her palm, and stared at him with resignation. "What do you need?"

"Nothing much, just, um..." He forgot what he was going to ask her to do, now that he'd made up his mind to keep her on and given himself a dozen excuses why he should, because all his brain wanted was to have that temptress smile back at him one more time. He couldn't do that though, he couldn't encourage her to want him, then turn her down.

Even if the young geek he'd once been wanted that more than anything.

"Well?" She asked and sat back in the booth, efficient and ready to take notes, even if it was mental notes.

"Nothing, really, don't worry about it. We'll do it tomorrow. Just relax tonight. You deserve it."

"Oh. Thanks, Logan." She leaned back against the booth and when the waiter brought their pie over, she ate it quietly but quickly. Regret gnawed at him that she wanted to get away from him now. "I guess I need to get going then."

"Oh, uh, yes, I suppose you do. I'll walk you out to your car." He left some money on the table that should be more than enough to cover their bill and walked out with her. The quiet solitude of the restaurant disappeared as the sounds of the town's nightlife reached them. A band was playing somewhere nearby, and vehicles zoomed up and down the road. "It's busier here at night than I thought it would be."

"It's not too bad, but sometimes I miss living in a bigger city. Back when Joe was, I mean we were at school, we lived on campus, in a big town and the nightlife was amazing. It's a lot quieter here." She smiled up at him, her face illuminated by a streetlamp. Her eyes gleamed in the darkness and the way she tilted her head beckoned him closer as she leaned against her car.

She'd parked close to the front doors and Logan kind of wished she'd parked somewhere darker, more secluded. Somewhere where he could pull her body up against his and kiss her without curious eyes following every move they made.

It was obvious she wanted him to kiss her when she leaned back against the car and tilted her face up to his, her eyes full of a dare he couldn't take. She was a liar and dangerous, he reminded himself. Dangerous to his peace of mind and his business. He was well aware that she could take everything away from him with one single sexual harassment claim and as much as he might want Keily, he couldn't risk losing his business.

Instead of kissing her lips, he skimmed her jaw with his lips, whispered goodnight to her, ignored the shiver of need that ran through her, and walked away. It might have been a mistake to hire her but sleeping with her would be an even bigger mistake. One he couldn't afford to make.

13

Keily

"*H*ello?" Rosa's voice filled her car as she drove away from the restaurant, a curious, disembodied voice that made Keily smile. "How'd it go? You're calling me and it's barely past 9:30 so I know it didn't end in seduction. Unless he's one of those two-pumps kind of guys. Oh no, he's not is he?"

"No." Keily drawled out slowly but with a giggle in her throat. "Well, not that I know of anyway. He walked me to my car and that was it."

"But you were alone with him, your text said," Rosa replied and Keily could hear her washing dishes in the background.

"We were." Keily sighed and turned off onto the next road she had to take to get home. "He'd run off to the bathroom when I sent that, but he wasn't gone long. He was acting strange."

"How do you mean?" Rosa prompted and the sound of running water stopped.

"Well, he was just - nervous or something. Not his normal confident self." Keily shook her head even though Rosa couldn't see her. "And I could swear I've met him before."

"Huh?" Rosa blurted and Keily grinned in the darkness.

"Déjà vu hit me pretty hard, but I don't know where I know him from."

"High school maybe? Aren't you both from here?"

"No, I didn't go to a school with a guy like Logan, I'd remember him." She was certain of that.

"So, maybe he was at another school? Isn't there another one on the other side of the county?"

"There is," Keily answered and thought Rosa must be right. "That would explain how I don't know him. Our paths rarely crossed, the kids from my high school and that one."

"There you go then," Rosa responded and Keily was sure the other woman had just opened a bottle of wine. She'd heard a cork pop.

"Maybe that's all it is. Anyway, nothing happened, and I wasn't fired, which is always an accomplishment as far as I'm concerned."

"Such a waste." Rosa sighed before she went on. "That man really needs to get laid, and so do you, young lady."

"I know, but I'm not sure it needs to be with each other. Even if I wouldn't mind if it was." She laughed loudly over that and pulled to a stop at a stoplight.

"I can only live through you. The man has no interest in me whatsoever. Which is probably a good thing, because I really like having you as a friend. I wouldn't want a man to come between us." Rosa's voice trailed off just as Keily put her foot back down on the gas pedal.

"Even if he did make a move on you, and you accepted, I wouldn't blame you, Rosa. He's fucking hot. Even if he is the world's biggest asshole." Keily couldn't help but shake her head over her own stupidity. "I know I shouldn't be interested at all in him, I just can't help it, though. Even when he makes me feel like I'm an inch tall."

"The things we do, right?" Rosa made a tsk noise before she carried on. "Well, keep me updated, maybe he'll realize how stupid he was in letting you go tonight."

"I'll definitely keep you updated," Keily answered with a soft laugh, realizing that she was almost home, and the call was almost over. "I doubt anything will happen, he's determined to keep it platonic, but you never know."

"Maybe he's worried about a lawsuit," Rosa said

suddenly and Keily knew the conversation wasn't quite over yet. "I can't say that I blame him for being careful, but I also don't think you'd ever do anything that wasn't right."

Keily wasn't sure she'd always have done the right thing, but she was a new person now. Not the one that had nearly stolen from her baby niece, or the person she'd been in high school definitely. The one her mother had paraded with so much glee from pageant to pageant until Keily hated the idea of more pageants. She'd even come to resent her mom over the stupid things eventually, but at the same time, those pageants, and her mother, had given her a reason to hold her head up high for a long time.

"No, I wouldn't do something like that," Keily reassured her friend. She might have, out of spite a long time ago, but she'd grown up a lot over the last few weeks.

She might have once been the queen of the high school and had the most popular friends, but that was all gone now. She hadn't cared who she hurt back then, but it was all high school stuff. Nobody took any of their pranks or the things they said seriously, right? They all knew it was just that, high school bullshit.

"I might have been a complete bitch in high school, but I'm not that girl anymore. I know what it's like to stand on my own two feet now, to take care of myself, and I'm far more proud of that than I will ever be of some cheap crown I might have won a long time ago."

"I can't imagine you being a mean girl, Keily," Rosa said before she took a sip of whatever was in her glass. "Maybe a little snarky, but never one of those awful mean girls."

"I was a cheerleader," Keily answered in a moment of rare self-awareness. "And my mom forced me to always look perfect, act perfect, be perfect. She didn't do that shit with my sister, so she just doesn't get me, she thinks I'm spoiled, but yeah, Mom made me what I was. And I might not have exactly been the most terrible kid out there, but I wasn't very nice, either."

"That's really honest of you, Keily." Rosa paused as if thinking. "I don't think that's who you are now, at all. I don't even think that's who you might have been, really."

"You're kind to say that, but I can be honest with myself about it now. I wasn't nice, at all." Keily didn't want to admit it, but it was true. And even if she didn't want to admit it, she could now. She hadn't even been nice a few months ago.

It was only since she'd had to get a job and support herself that she realized she treated people terribly. Even her own family. Now she knew, and it was time to find a way to make up for that. If that meant being someone different than she'd always been, then so be it.

She'd thought she needed to marry Joe, have babies,

and be a football wife to feel like she'd achieved her mother's dreams. The fact that her mom was still upset with her for divorcing Joe told her all she needed to know about how her mom felt about the way that had all fallen apart. Her mother had raised her two daughters differently, and Keily wasn't sure why, but she suspected it had something to do with her mother's own childhood, not hers.

So many deep thoughts tonight, she laughed to herself, she'd be seeking out a psychiatrist next. "I'm no angel, Rosa, but I can try to be one from now on."

"Well, you've been nothing but nice to me, so I don't want to hear any more about it. You almost home?"

"I am, so I'm going to get off of here and get out of this dress. You coming over tomorrow evening, still?" She asked, just to confirm the dinner they had planned.

It was one of the ways she was trying to improve herself, trying new dishes and having Rosa test them.

"You know I love whatever you cook so plan to have an extra-large plate for me," Rosa said with a snort.

"I've got one just for you." Keily pulled into her parking space, turned the car off, and looked around as the phone went back to speakerphone instead of playing through the car's speaker system. "It's quiet here tonight."

"No kitties at the door tonight?"

"Not a single one, and no old man in boxers and an

open robe on his front stoop either." Keily shrugged, grabbed her bag, and got out of the car with her keys in her other hand.

"If I hadn't had a glass of wine I'd come over and keep you company, but I have."

"It's alright, I'm in the door now and going straight to bed." She'd take off her makeup and brush her teeth, but she didn't need to say that.

"Sounds like a plan. I'll talk to you tomorrow then." Rosa took another sip of her wine.

"Laters, tater," Keily said jokingly, closed her door, locked it, and then put her bag and keys down. Rosa said her own goodbye and Keily put the phone down to head into the bathroom.

She'd really hoped that Logan had other plans for tonight but at the same time, she was kind of glad things hadn't gone that way. She liked him, yes, found him attractive and funny when he wasn't being an asshole, but she still barely knew him.

And he was her boss, she reminded herself for the millionth time. She looked into her own eyes as she scrubbed her makeup off and applied moisturizer. It would be insanely boring for her to sleep with her boss. Wouldn't it?

Her dreams told her differently, but fantasies and dreams had a way of making us believe lies, if we let them, she decided. He was probably a selfish, arrogant prick in bed too, the kind that paid lip service to getting a woman off but couldn't tell if he actually had or not. Like Joe. She'd had more pleasure out of her vibrator than she'd out of him throughout their years in high school and the ones after, when they were married.

Maybe it was because he'd had little experience? Now that could be it, she thought as she brushed her teeth. Logan looked like a man that had been around a little, the kind that could probably blow her socks off if he applied himself.

She grinned, put on her pajamas, and headed to her bed to watch something to fall asleep to. She found a new movie on her streaming service and turned it on but regretted it the second a handsome man with broody eyes came on her screen. He didn't compare with Logan, and she laughed more in the first three minutes of the film than she had all day.

She tried to imagine Logan saying some of the incredibly corny things the film's main male character said and just couldn't fathom it. It didn't matter if the man was exotic, had a sexy accent, and a body that men would envy, he just wasn't Logan. Sure, she could appreciate the fact that the actor was hot, but was he Logan hot?

Nope, not at all, she decided and settled into the comforter with her face away from the television. There weren't many men on the planet that could compare with Logan. If you wanted a jerk, that is, she grumped to herself as sleep started to take over. A jerk with beautiful brown eyes that haunted her right up until her dreams started and she felt his hands on her skin. Then those eyes tormented her as they demanded she come for him, over and over again. But even then, despite the torment, she smiled in her dreams because he was doing exactly what she wanted him to do.

THE NEXT MORNING it was hard to wake up, even with her alarm clock. She had two cups of coffee before she went out to her car and all that did was make her run for the bathroom with a bladder screaming at her by the time she got to the office. Another cup didn't help, and by lunchtime, she was ready for a nap. If it wasn't so hot out, she'd go to her car and take a nap.

Instead, she went out with Rosa to have a chef salad for lunch. Instead of her normal light salad dressing, she piled on thick, creamy, totally fattening ranch dressing. She ate every bite with pure delight. The once-in-a-blue-moon treat didn't help her wake up but it did make her smile.

"What's wrong with you today?" Rosa pressed after she'd finished her roast beef sandwich.

"Nothing, I don't know. I don't feel bad, I'm just

tired." She pushed the empty plate away and brushed her hands through her hair. "Too many vivid dreams, I guess."

"Oh, do tell…" Rosa teased, her eyes full of glee.

"The usual," Keily said dismissively, too tired to go over the same dreams she'd had before.

"He's keeping you awake, even in your dreams." Rosa laughed again and leaned back in her chair. "If you don't feel like making dinner tonight, I can bring pizza or a lasagna over."

"Hmm, don't tempt me." Keily frowned down at the plate, hating how she'd suddenly decided to eat her feelings. "How can dreams make you so damn tired."

"I guess it's what you do in those dreams that does it." Rosa countered and then went on. "I hate the ones where you wake up afraid someone has died, or angry at someone even more."

"Oh, I've had those with Joe." Keily shook her head. "I used to dream he was having affairs all the time and I'd be mad at him for days."

They both laughed at that and people turned to look at them. Keily couldn't even rouse the energy to glare back. She enjoyed the dreams, but this exhaustion was just too much when it hadn't even been the real thing.

Later, when she was back in the office with Logan, she stared at him with the glare she hadn't been able to muster earlier.

Who the hell was he, and why had he seemed familiar last night? She watched him move around the office until he went in and closed the door to his private office. When she heard him on the phone, she opened her browser window and searched for his name. A very old Facebook page, an Instagram page for the company, and a few of those places that will sell you people's public records for more than they're worth came up. She frowned at the results and then typed his name and California into the search bar.

That showed quite a few newspaper and magazine articles but didn't reveal a lot about him or his personal life. Not anything worth reading at all.

She tapped her short fingernails against her desk and stared off into space. There had to be more about Logan out there. None of the things she found went back to anything before he was eighteen years old, not even the public records. Maybe he was lying about being from King's Hill, she thought suddenly.

Maybe he was Canadian or something had changed his accent and made up a story to be one of the locals. No, that was too much work for not a lot of gain, if any really. No, that couldn't be it. It also wouldn't explain why he seemed familiar. As in she knew him familiar, not like she'd seen him on television or even the internet or in pictures familiar. Like she'd seen that look live and in person before.

And that meant she'd met him before. But he'd never given her a clue that he'd been anywhere near her before he came back to this town. Maybe she'd met him at a restaurant or something a long time ago, before he went off to get a degree and became rich? That would make sense, more sense than he was Canadian and lying about it.

With a dismissive laugh, she closed the browser window and answered the phone when it rang. There was a problem down in the factory and Logan would have to go down to see to it. She sighed as she got up out of her chair and knocked on his door. Another day, another dollar, she told herself. A few more hours and she could relax with Rosa and a bottle of wine on her sofa. And if she was lucky, there'd be no dreams about Logan tonight. Even if she might miss those dreams, a little.

14

Keily

"Girl, if you eyeball fuck him any harder either the room is going to catch fire or HR will be on your case for sexual harassment." Rosa's voice paused, then a giggle came out of the other bathroom stall next to Keily. "Wait, that's me."

Keily smiled and rolled her eyes good-naturedly.

"You drink anymore and you're going to fall off the toilet, Rosa," Keily muttered, her eyes on the stall door of the restaurant washrooms they were all in.

All meant everyone from work. Including Logan. She pulled the right corner of her mouth up in a frown and wondered who Tania was and what she'd done to be called a whore by an anonymous scribbler. Keily tried not to think about how many other hands had touched the light blue painted door and continued to read. Finished with her business, she got up, flushed the toilet, took her bag from the peg on the door, and went out to wash her hands.

"I can't believe a place as fancy as this has such grubby stalls," Rosa said as she buckled her belt then washed her own hands.

Keily, her hands under an air dryer, turned with an *I know* look on her face. "There's writing on the doors too. It's like being in school all over again."

"The only thing missing is the feminine hygiene product dispenser." Rosa waved at the empty walls.

"We didn't have those in my high school, but I remember my mom asking me about them when I was in school and had an unexpected arrival. I tried to call her to come and bring me some tampons and she asked me about the dispenser." Keily rolled her eyes and waited for Rosa to dry her own hands.

"I grew up in a poor county, they made their money any way they could," Rosa said as an off-hand comment but Keily noticed.

"Was it bad?" She asked softly, not wanting to upset her friend but curious.

"Not terrible, we just didn't always have some of the stuff city kids had or some of the things larger school districts had. We had a lot of military recruiters at my school if that tells you anything."

"No, what do you mean?" Keily asked, her left brow furrowed as she stared back at the one friend, she would trust above anyone else now. Even Violet.

"They tend to target poor school districts. Some would say they don't, but I saw it, still do. They go into those schools and offer kids the moon. I don't know if they ever make good on those promises, my brother says not. He was in the Marines for eight years before he called it quits and got out." Rosa brushed hair out of her eyes, adjusted the waist of the black skirt she had on, fluffed out the white blouse she wore with it, and turned to Keily with a smile. "Anyway, I like that red dress. Is it new?"

"Yeah, old habits die hard." Keily held out her hands so Rosa could inspect the red dress she'd bought for the company Christmas party. It was a close-fitting cotton dress with long sleeves, a long hemline that came down to mid-calf, but featured black buttons down the front with a very deep V over the cleavage. "I can't believe it's Christmas already."

"We've worked for Logan for five months now." Rosa sighed, leaned back against a sink, not in a rush to go back out. "You still dreaming about him?"

Keily didn't mind that her friend was settling in for a chat. She wasn't eager to get back out there and watch women throw themselves at Logan either. After that night at the restaurant, Keily had tried to forget how

Logan made her feel and do her job. It was those damn dreams that wouldn't leave her alone.

She tried to forget the dreams and had attempted to exhaust herself at night by coming home and swimming, which had been great for her physique before it got too cold to swim and they closed the pool, but did little to stop her dreaming about the man. Rosa knew about the dreams because Keily told her about them over too much wine one night.

They'd made a pact since then not to drink so much, which they'd stuck to, kind of. It wasn't every week like it used to be anyway, Keily thought with a secret smile that Rosa mistook.

"You *are* still dreaming about him, aren't you?" Rosa leaned forward, away from the sink to look up into Keily's face. "You arrrre!"

"I am. I can't help it. He's a complete and utter asshole but when he's quiet and doesn't say anything, or he comes up behind me and just *breathes*, like he can't make up his mind if he wants to walk past me or bend me over and fuck me, I just want to tear his clothes off." Keily joined Rosa in leaning against another sink and sighed deeply.

"I know I shouldn't say this because I *am* HR, but you have to do something about this. Pull him off to a corner, climb into his car and bang him on his backseat, I don't care what you do, but I've been watching this develop for five months now. You two are going to explode, one way or another, and it will be messy if you don't watch out." Rosa's face moved into a serious look, almost a frown, before she continued. "Get it out of your system and get it over with."

"I would if he'd let me." Keily groaned and let her head fall back. "I don't get it. One minute he's on the verge of kissing me, the next he's telling me he hates the way I crinkle papers when I'm going through the company's mail at my desk, sorting it for him."

"I know what I'd do." Rosa giggled again, and it was obvious that they'd both maybe decided it was one of those weeks where they'd have a little too much to drink.

Logan had already said he'd pay for a taxi for anybody that needed a ride home tonight, so it wasn't a bad thing. Just two women, letting their hair down on their boss's dime. Keily giggled as she thought about Logan out there fending off the two elderly ladies that worked in the sales office. They adored him and it was more than obvious they wanted to mother him. It wasn't mothering that she wanted to do with him. Not at all.

Maybe *become* a mother with him, and with that, she sputtered out a laugh and pulled Rosa from the bathroom with her. "Let's get back out there and see if I still have any magic left."

"Girl, you're only 25…"

"Ah-ah! 26 next week." Keily interrupted.

"I can't believe you were born on Christmas Eve," Rosa answered, her left arm through Keily's right.

"Well, it kind of makes Christmas suck but Mom always said I was her Christmas miracle." Keily shrugged and smiled at her friend. "I had two days of presents, but still, it was all so close together that it was like I only had one birthday or one Christmas."

"That sucks," Rosa said, gasped in surprise at what she'd said, then looked over at Keily in apology. "I guess it actually does suck, doesn't it?"

"It does, but it's okay."

There were fewer people by the time they got back to their table and Keily was a little sad to see the party winding down. That meant she'd have to go home to her quiet apartment sooner than she wanted to. She turned to Rosa, busy pouring wine into their glasses, and frowned.

"You want to come back to my place tonight? We can get up in the morning and go sightseeing or something." Keily didn't want to sound desperate for companion-ship, she still had some pride, but she didn't want to be alone either.

"I'm going to my Mom's in the morning," Rosa said with an apologetic look. "Remember, I'm going to her house for Christmas?"

"Yes, sorry, I forgot for a moment why we were

here." Keily brushed the refusal off with a laugh and leaned back in the black chair that wasn't really comfortable but looked attractive in pictures. "I'll just look at my Christmas tree, then, and watch *Frosty the Snowman* with a cup of hot chocolate."

"Put some crème de menthe in it. It tastes like heaven." Rosa sighed and looked over at Keily. "Listen, I'm going to head home. I need to get up early and if I leave you here alone long enough Logan might get up the nerve to come over here and talk to you and stop staring at us both."

Keily glanced around, looking for the man that infuriated her completely, but also confused her completely. How could she be so attracted to a man that habitually told her, in no uncertain terms, that she was doing a poor job? It was like he was on a mission to break her, even if he had calmed down a little lately and wasn't such a bully.

Her brows drew down as she caught his eyes and her head tilted back towards Rosa. "You're right. He's probably trying to think up some new way to ruin my night with work. Maybe I should head home too?"

"No, you stay. Try to get this out of your system by the time I come back to King's Hill. Or else the whole place will go nuclear and all that work that Logan's done to improve the place will be obliterated."

"He has done a lot for the town." Keily agreed, which

was another point in his favor. He'd saved the dying town, given people jobs, and brought new life to the town that was once on the verge of becoming a ghost town. That was one reason she could see him in a good light, she thought as she continued to stare at him.

"That's not the point. Sex. Over Christmas. Or else!" Rosa leaned over to kiss Keily's cheek; the full glass of wine forgotten on the table. "I will be back."

"Oh, don't start your bad movie quotes." Keily sputtered, trying to talk and laugh at the same time. "Call me when you've settled in at your mom's."

"I will. And you call me if anything happens." Rosa grabbed her bag from under the table and stood up. "Even if it's the middle of the night."

"I will. Merry Christmas, honey. I hope you have a wonderful time at your mom's. I'll miss you."

"I'll miss you too, and Merry Christmas." Rosa leaned over once more, hugged Keily, and turned to leave.

Keily watched her go, confused about why her eyes suddenly filled with tears at the thought of not seeing her friend for five more days. Then she thought about Violet and Alice, and how Violet still didn't want to talk to her and something that might be grief closed her throat up as the tears fell from her eyes.

Loneliness, that's what it was. But she was Keily Matthews, she reminded herself as she picked up her glass of wine and swallowed it one gulp. She didn't need anybody, right?

Her eyes slowly tracked back to Logan, who was now talking to one of the shift managers from the plant. She quickly turned back around, picked up the glass Rosa had left, and gulped that one down too. He was such a…dick.

He'd smirked at her so quickly that she doubted anyone else saw it. And now he was walking over to her.

"Do you want me to call you a cab, Keily?"

"What? Why would I do that?" She wobbled a little in her seat and thought that might be why he'd asked her that question. Maybe she'd had too much.

"You're not in any state to drive. Alternatively, I could drive you home." The way he looked down at her with eyes full of hunger and something she couldn't identify made her head swim a little.

"Sure. That sounds great." She said stupidly and grabbed her bag from under the table. Rosa had said to get this over with. Well, she had the courage to be her old self again. It was now or never.

He'd offered her a ride home. She planned to offer so much more in return.

15

Logan

"Thanks for driving me home. I'd have called my sister but she's not talking to me right now. She'd only give me a lecture anyway." Keily drawled as he poured her into the expensive car he still loved.

If she puked in the car, he'd kill her, he thought. But then again, she's drunk and he'd offered, he reminded himself. He'd pay to have it cleaned if she couldn't hold the last two glasses of wine he'd watched her guzzle down.

She was obviously upset about something, but he suspected former cheerleaders often were. Yes, she'd come a long way since he'd met the cocky woman with hips that swaggered around like she owned the world, but underneath all of that, she was still the former cheerleader who had no idea what to do with herself.

"Why is your sister mad at you?" He asked to break the silence as he got into his seat and started the engine.

"Because I was a bitch to her, why else would she be mad?" Keily sputtered, and he knew she had no idea he didn't know her sister at all. "I mean, she's great, perfect, the kind of perfect Mom tried to make me, but she's the real deal."

"What do you mean?" He asked as he reversed the car and then headed out to the street.

"She's so damn *nice*. And loving. And all I ever did was give her grief." Keily slumped against the window, her seatbelt digging into her neck.

Logan thought he should probably move her off the restraint but then decided to leave her. She was upset, drunk and upset. That's usually what happened when people had too much to drink.

"I'm going to be alone for Christmas." She said after a few minutes of silence and after they'd passed three traffic lights that were magically all green at the same time.

"I'm sorry to hear that. I'm going to California." He was sorry that she'd be alone, despite her past and who she'd presented herself as, despite the fact that she'd lied to him about her education and work history, he liked Keily.

She worked hard and didn't complain unless she was drunk, he thought with a chuckle. He turned onto a street that was dark and lonely, careful to keep his eyes on the road. It was late and he was always a careful driver.

"Even you have family to go home to!" She cried even harder now, and he reached in the center console for a forgotten napkin to hand to her. He had a bad habit of stuffing unused napkins in there, so he had plenty to hand her.

"What do you mean? Your parents won't be here for Christmas?" He didn't look at her, just kept his eyes on the road and dimmed his lights when a car approached them from the opposite side of the road.

"No, they're in fucking Florida and won't even come up to see their granddaughter for Christmas. How messed up is that?" She moaned a little but wiped at her eyes and nose with the napkin.

"That's pretty messed up." Logan agreed and glanced at her. He'd braked at a stop sign and saw she was gaining control of herself finally. "You can always call your sister and apologize to her."

"Oh, I've tried. We've made a truce, sort of, but she's still angry with me." Keily started to cry again and turned to him with the saddest gray eyes he'd ever seen. "I just want her to love me again."

"She will." He answered, but had no idea if it was true

or not. He just wanted her to calm down a little before she made herself sick. "You'll see, before long you'll be back in her good graces. You're charming enough, you'll figure it out."

"I keep trying to mend everything with her, but I'm so busy all the time, I just don't have time to go and see her or my niece." She turned away and he knew she was blaming him for that.

And she was right to, he realized as he drove the long way around town. He wanted her to sober up a little before he got her back to her apartment. He also wanted to spend a little time with her alone.

He knew what would happen when he stopped in front of her apartment and maybe he wanted to put that off for a little while too. He was going to take Ms. Miller home, make sure she walked into her apartment safely, and then go home himself. He had no intentions of kissing her or fucking her.

He couldn't. He was her boss.

Still.

He replayed the same thoughts in his head that he had a million times already while she leaned back against the car seat. Her eyes closed as he drove to an all-night fast food place and ordered two coffees. She sat up when the smell of the coffee filled the car and took her cup.

"That smells too good to be true." She sipped it

slowly, her eyes still closed. With a sigh, she sat back in the seat again and smiled.

She did know how to enjoy the simple things in life then. Good.

Keily finished the coffee just as he pulled up in front of her apartment and got out of the car. He took the empty cup from her and put it back in the cupholder when she forgot how to undo her seatbelt with the cup in her hands. "I'll throw that away, don't worry Keily."

"Thanks." She giggled, grabbed her bag, and got out of the car.

It was a short distance to her door and before he knew it, she was turning back to him with her keys in her hand. He could see the question in her eyes just as her lips pursed to ask him. He was ready to refuse, not only was she his employee, she was drunk, and he would not take advantage of a woman incapable of making good decisions.

Even if his body screamed at him to just get it over with already, that it was the one thing on this planet that he wanted above anything else. Which was an entirely different reason to turn down the proposal, but he didn't get to finish that thought because instead of asking him, Keily leaned over and kissed him.

She tasted of the coffee she'd just had and a mint she'd popped into her mouth at some point. It wasn't unpleasant, and he really didn't care, not when her tongue was teasing at his lips, demanding he open for her. She was a woman who knew what she wanted then.

He allowed the kiss, for now, certain he could pull away at any moment. He had control of himself. Well, he did right up until she pressed her breasts into his chest and he felt her hips tuck against his body. Her arms went around his waist and he couldn't stop himself.

With a groan of surrender, he took her chin in his right hand and held her face still so he could kiss her properly, taste her properly. When her body sagged into his a little deeper, and she groaned, he knew the decision was made and damned the consequences. She tasted like the heaven she would bring and the promises her body made were all he'd ever wanted, all he didn't know he wanted because he'd never had Keily Matthews Miller pressed into him like this before.

Faintly, he heard a car pull into one of the parking spaces that ran along the front of the building, but he ignored it. He nudged her back against the door, ready to give her everything he had to give her, every thick inch of him. The way she clutched at his wool coat, tugged him to her, told him she wanted this, and it was more than just a drunken surrender to the attraction between them, neither of them could fight it anymore.

"Come inside, Logan." She pulled away long enough to whisper and he was about to agree, about to give in to his own body's demands, when he heard a voice behind him.

"Hey! Asshole!" A male voice, an angry voice that confused Logan. Who the hell was calling him asshole?

"I'm sorry, what's your problem?" But Logan didn't get to turn all the way around before a sledgehammer punched him in the face. At least, that's what it felt like when it met the left side of his face.

"She's my wife, dipshit. Get the fuck off her." Logan could hear a slur to the voice as he tried to get his ears to stop ringing.

He dropped to the concrete stoop in front of Keily's door when the man sucker-punched him, but now he slowly got up. Carefully, he pulled a slim black device from his pocket and waited to see what would happen next.

As he suspected, the man launched himself at Keily next and she screamed as she kicked out at him with the pointed black stilettos he loved so much. She swung her bag at him at the same time and the man stumbled back. He'd love those shoes even more from now on, he decided as the man screamed in pain when the point met his testicles.

"Keily, you fucking whore! What the fuck, man?" He groaned as he got up again.

"Joe, leave me alone. Go the fuck home! Why are you still doing this? We're divorced, stop stalking me. Fuck, why can't you leave me alone? I thought we were done with this bullshit." Keily glared at her ex and Logan turned back to the man.

"Go home, Joe. She's not your wife anymore." Logan tried to say but Joe, his face bloated from years of too many beers and not enough nutrition, launched himself at Logan again. Logan was ready for him and as Joe got close enough, Logan pushed the black device he'd cradled in his hand into Joe's abdomen.

Joe dropped like a stone instantly and wailed in pain.

Logan rolled his eyes. "Call the cops, Keily. Now."

"Of course, Logan." She answered, clearly embarrassed because she wouldn't look him in the eye. "He's been stalking me since I left him, but after our divorce was finalized, I thought he'd stopped. Now he shows up tonight…"

"It's okay, Keily. Just call the cops. He attacked both of us. I'm not having it." Logan stared down at the former quarterback, now little more than a man with a busted knee and no hopes or dreams.

This was the kind of guy that had tormented him all through his earlier years. It was Joe and pricks like him that had scarred him, mentally and physically, with their attacks. He'd dropped the guy, not with a punch but with a very small taser that he kept in his hand, in case the asshole got up again. "Stay down, Joe, for your own good."

Joe took the warning for what it was, mainly because he was too stunned to get up. It wasn't that the device was so powerful it could cause that much shock; it was that he was drunk and had been tased at the same time. Stay the fuck down, he thought at the slob. How long has he had those clothes on? Logan wondered with a sneer of distaste. He reeked of body odor and beer.

"They'll be here in just a minute, there's a patrol car at the end of the street already," Keily said to him, still not willing to meet his eyes.

Because of that kiss, her inebriation, both of those, or because of Joe? Maybe it was all three he decided and leaned back against the wall of her apartment. "We left your coat at the restaurant. I'll pick it up tomorrow. Why don't you go in, Keily, and get out of the cold?"

The way she looked up at him finally, with so much regret and the last dregs of desire, made his body go rock hard. He'd almost given in to her, to his own desire, but Joe had put a stop to that.

"I'll be fine, go on in." He nodded at the door and watched as she turned to go back into the house.

"I'll come back out when the cops get here." She promised and then put her key into the lock.

He waited until she'd closed the door before he turned back to Joe. The former all-star quarterback was now a waste of space.

"Listen, Joe, this is how it's going to be. I'm going to press charges against you." He crouched down low enough to look Joe in the face. The man was still on the ground, moaning and crying. "I'm going to win, because unlike when we were all in high school, I'm the one that calls the shots now. You're a loser who lost everything, including a woman who was probably an amazing wife to you."

He could hear the sounds of the sirens as Joe groaned and turned to look at him with bleary eyes. He didn't have long, he had to get his point across to the guy before they got here.

"You're going to take your punishment, and you're going to leave Keily alone too, do you understand me?" Logan could see the defeat on the man's face and smiled a very happy smile.

Joe started to protest when he saw Logan's smile, but Logan didn't let him. "You think because you played football in high school and college that the world owes you something? You played a useless game that didn't actually achieve anything for the world, got fucked up doing it, and now you want what I have. I worked for my life, asshole, and I'll be damned if someone like you comes in and tries to take anything from me ever again. I'll ruin you even more than you've already ruined yourself."

Joe's head went back down to the ground, before he

tried to stand up, but couldn't get to his feet. He was too drunk for anything like coordination.

"Stay down, Joe, because if you don't, I have much stronger tasers than that. They won't kill you, but you'll wish you were dead by the time I'm finished with you."

"Is that a threat?" Joe finally spoke again, his eyes narrowed. The cocky asshole was back then.

Logan dipped his head down to the ground for a minute. He didn't need this shit; he didn't need it at all. But it was incredible knowing that he was finally getting control over a bully like Joe.

"No, my friend, it's a promise. One you can bet your life on. Leave her alone. Leave me alone. Or else." The steely resolve in Logan's gaze must have convinced the man because he scrambled up from the ground and all but ran to the cops to beg them to take him to jail.

What a man, Logan thought with a smirk as the cops climbed out of their car and grabbed Joe. What a waste of space. Logan rolled his eyes and headed over to the cops. He'd get this over with then head back to his house. Going to California might actually be a relief for a change. He'd get away from this mess he'd made, even if it was only for a little while.

16

Keily

*K*eily spent Christmas and New Year's Eve alone, trying to think of a way to apologize to her sister and to Logan. She'd thrown herself at him after the company Christmas party and she hadn't heard from him since. As for her sister, well, nothing she thought of seemed right.

She'd sent gifts to her sister's house for Alice and Violet but hadn't even received a thank you text. Nothing. And she knew the presents were delivered because she'd got the tracking notifications. As the hours slipped away into days, Keily decided that perhaps her sister would never forgive her and maybe she deserved it.

Logan was a totally different problem.

Between what Joe did and the fact that she'd embarrassed herself by getting drunk and kissing him all whirled into something that Keily thought might be shame. She didn't want to feel it, but it ate at her anyway. Joe had been a complete idiot when she left him, and he'd made life miserable for her for a long time.

He'd followed her around town, managed to find ways to get her phone number to call her constantly, begging her to come back, even when she'd changed her number three different times. She'd finally given up on that working and kept her number after the last time she'd seen his number come up on her phone.

It had been hard, a little scary, but mainly annoying.

She'd left him after he humiliated her and himself. Not just within the community but in the larger viewing area of the news station he worked for.

Keily pushed that memory away as she got out of the elevator and walked into the office. Logan hadn't called her, texted her, or anything else since he'd left her apartment that night. She'd been sober by the time the police questioned her about what had happened and agreed to be a witness for Logan.

He hadn't even sent her an email. She'd checked her phone constantly, but nothing ever came up. Even when she made Christmas dinner for one, a sad affair of a very small roast chicken, a box of stuffing, a tiny can of green beans, and a pack of instant mashed potatoes, she checked her phone. When she rang in the new year alone, with a small glass of wine because Rosa decided to stay at her mom's house for that too, she checked her phone.

Now, it was the third of January and time to get back to work.

Logan's door was closed when she reached her desk, but she saw a printed sheet of paper taped to her computer monitor. She stopped, closed her eyes, took a deep breath, and tried not to cringe. Not this shit again.

Keily,

Get me coffee and bring it to my office by 9:15.

For lunch, I want lasagna from that place across the street.

At 3:15 I have a meeting with a buyer, show her in as soon as she arrives.

Don't fuck up anything today, or it will be the last day you work for me.

Logan.

Keily put her bag down, took out her wallet, and headed out to get Logan coffee. It was 8:30 she should have time to get his coffee and bring it back to him. While she stood in line, he sent her an email that contained a letter he wanted her to type up and print out. It was a picture of a handwritten letter. His handwriting was neat, always cursive, and easy to read.

It wasn't long and probably took more effort to write out and photograph, then email, than it would have taken if he'd just typed the damn thing up himself. She rolled her eyes, took the coffee for him, as well as one for her, along with a sausage biscuit, and left the café.

Twenty minutes later, after she'd dropped off his coffee in his office without a word, she'd had her biscuit and her coffee and was typing the letter he'd sent her. Her back tensed when she heard his door open and he walked out of his office.

"What's this?" He asked as he came to a stop beside her.

"The coffee you wanted." She said with a slight frown. Had the café staff messed up?

"I wanted a latte, not a regular coffee." He said quietly before he let the coffee drop into her wastebasket. "Go get me the right coffee, Keily. Fuck, why can't you pay attention?"

He left the outer office and went back into his private office.

She had paid attention. She'd checked the note he'd left her before she went down to the café. One regular coffee, that's what he'd asked for. But it was Logan. He could play stupid games when he wanted to.

Please, not this shit again. For a second, her head slumped over her desk and she wanted to cry. How long would it be this time?

Was his attitude punishment for kissing him or for Joe attacking him?

She'd sent him an email the day after the party, an apology for her and Joe's behavior, but he'd never responded.

While she took the elevator down, she thought about Christmas Eve, her birthday, and how she'd spent it alone. She'd managed to buy a single cupcake from the local bakery and had taken it home to have dinner alone. She did get a text from Rosa and a phone call from her parents, but that was all.

She'd been so lonely that she went to bed early, too depressed to stay awake to watch a movie or anything else. She'd just gone to bed, turned out the lights, and slept the rest of the day away. She had no presents under her tree, nobody to spend the next day with.

Now Logan was back to his cranky boss routine.

Maybe it was because he'd lost control of himself before Joe punched him.

She might have been drunk when she leaned over to kiss him, but she remembered every moment of having his lips pressed to hers, of being in his arms. She'd seen the denial on his lips as she started to ask him in and had decided to take a chance and kiss him instead. It had been an impulsive decision and one she wouldn't have made without the alcohol, of course, but she didn't regret doing it.

Nobody had ever kissed her like that, not with that much passion. He'd groaned into her mouth when she slipped her arms around his waist, and she'd felt just how eager he was for her. There'd been no denying he was aroused, not from what she'd felt pressed against her. It was a very impressive sign of his arousal too. Joe had ruined it all, though.

She could have spent Christmas with Logan, her birthday too, maybe, if Logan had stayed that night, if Joe hadn't interrupted him. Or maybe he'd have pushed her away eventually and told her to back off. She didn't know if he'd have ended the kiss, if he'd have gone home the next morning without mentioning it ever again, and she never would now. Because Joe had taken that moment from her too.

If he wasn't so useless, she'd hate him too. But he was useless. He was an annoying, useless, embarrassing lump that refused to stay out of her life. Why wouldn't he just go away? Was she the only one he thought he could impress or something?

She'd stopped being impressed with him about the time she had to do his first major assignment because he was the star quarterback and couldn't take the time to do his own schoolwork. She'd earned his degree, not him. So why had she married him then?

It was a question she'd often wondered, even before she actually married him. Why Joe? Back then, it had been obvious. She'd wanted the power and wealth he'd bring to her as an NFL player. She wanted the glamor and fame of being his wife, a man that millions of women would want. Lucky for him, those women didn't know how bad he was in bed.

Keily went down in the elevator a second time that morning and brought back the latte Logan asked for. He promptly ignored it. And her.

She went back down again to get them both lunch and brought his back along with hers.

"Lasagna? I've had enough lasagna to last me a lifetime. Go back down and get me the roast chicken instead." He waved her off without even looking away from his monitor to register her fury.

She wanted to scream. She wanted to open the box and dump the contents out on his head. She wanted to pick up his stapler and smack him in the head with it, but she knew she couldn't. Instead, she calmly turned around, put her food on her desk, and walked out of the office.

It was a good thing she'd asked for a ham sandwich with plenty of lettuce and ranch dressing because it would have been cold by the time she got to sit down and eat. Logan took one look at the chicken, which looked really delicious, and decided he wanted the lasagna instead. But not the one sitting on her desk, which she offered to microwave. Oh no, he wanted a new one that was still hot.

A slight squeak of annoyance made it past the tight

grip she had on her lips and Logan looked up. "Is that a problem?"

"No, Logan, of course not. I'll be just a few minutes."

"Good, I'm starving. Go on, hurry up." He actually shooed her away this time. She really hated when he did that.

"I'm going." She said softly, too softly for him to hear. She'd learned her lesson long ago. She had to watch what she said when he was in a mood like this. Anything would set him off in a tirade she didn't feel like dealing with right now.

She was slower coming back, and it wasn't just that she'd made so many trips down for him already. It was because she was tired.

Tired of being alone.

Tired of her family avoiding her.

Tired of Joe's bullshit.

And tired of Logan treating her like she was inept.

She'd learned all those months ago to let a lot of things go. He was picking on her, yes, but it seemed to be some kind of game he enjoyed playing, not really about her skills or lack of. She'd spent a lot of time watching instructional videos, playing with software she hadn't used in years to relearn skills she'd learned when she'd done Joe's homework for him. She'd also learned to Google like a master. She could find things she'd never dreamed of looking up before and had learned how to weed out results she didn't want as well.

She did her job very well now, exactly the way he wanted her to and for a while, they'd become something of a team. She anticipated his wants and needs, learned to take care of him, and often reminded him he needed to eat or take a break. He'd calmed down and come to grips with the fact that he'd hired her.

Now, he was back to his old ways and she knew he knew too, that she had nowhere else to go. She felt trapped by what she had and what she didn't have. She didn't have a support system outside of work and she didn't have one within. Except for Rosa, of course.

Rosa was always a rock, but since she'd come back from her mom's, she was very quiet. Distant even. Something was wrong that she wasn't ready to talk about but Keily had told her only the night before that she was there for her friend. When and if she needed a shoulder, Keily would be there.

And she would be, she decided as she stepped into the street to the café, but she wouldn't pressure her friend to talk to her. Which meant that Rosa was still upset about whatever was on her mind and Keily didn't want to burden her further. Especially since it was an old complaint, one that even Keily was tired of complaining about.

Although the part about Joe was new. Kind of. It

would be new for Rosa, not for Keily. It was just one more problem to deal with.

A car blew its horn at her and Keily looked up, totally shocked to find a car less than a foot away from her, engine running. Had she stepped in front of it?

"Get out of the way, meth head!" A voice called from the driver's side window.

Keily frowned at the car, put her middle finger up, and continued to walk across the street. Fuck that guy.

And fuck Logan too.

She'd keep taking his money, do her job, and one day he'd be back to kissing her ass. And her.

Maybe.

He wouldn't be this way forever. She hoped.

And if he was, if this was how he was going to be from now on because of one kiss, and one pissed ex-husband, well, she'd just look for another job. Logan could really fuck off then. She pulled her head up a little higher as she stepped onto the curb on the other side of the street. She might even look for a job in another town. Or a city. Maybe even another state. She'd take a lesson from Rosa and say fuck you to them all. Maybe.

17

Logan

Why couldn't they go back to that night when her ex-husband showed up? Or before that even. He'd been dreading coming back to work since he left her that night and now, he felt like a complete douchebag. He'd treated her like dirt since she came in, but he wanted to put their relationship back on the rails.

They'd veered off from the professional relationship he'd cultivated quite carefully the night of the Christmas party. The workers in the plant had worked so hard that he'd given them two weeks off over Christmas and New Year's Eve. He had the California office handle any problems that popped up, but nothing had really gone wrong. Other than kissing Keily and tasing her ex.

He should thank Joe really. The man's brutal interruption had kept him from sleeping with Keily. That should be worth dropping the charges against the man. Even if his dick hated Joe for the interruption. And perhaps his brain did too.

He'd been plagued with dreams of her since that night. Christmas had been a blur of not paying attention, trying to pretend he was present when he clearly wasn't, and fending off thoughts about going back to South Carolina and the blonde beauty that haunted him. Even the dinner party Wally had given hadn't been enough to distract him. Logan had attended hoping to distract himself, but he'd failed miserably.

He watched Keily leave his office after he'd petulantly demanded a new lasagna and felt like a toad. He had to do it though. It was for her own good. She might want him, but she didn't want a man like him.

The boy he used to be would say it was the wealth he had, the power, that attracted Keily to him. That wasn't it though, and he knew it. She was lonely and yeah, she found him attractive, but there was something more between them. Something he refused to acknowledge.

They made a good team at work and that was all that really mattered. He handled his business and she had to handle hers. As long as she continued to do that, she'd have a job. Otherwise, he'd let her go. He'd have to. He couldn't keep her on if she did a bad job.

She didn't, to her credit. She'd learned fast and worked hard for him. He'd made sure of that.

Unlike her ex. The man was everything Logan hated about high school. Logan's hard work and brain had helped him get ahead. Joe had waited for the world to give him what he wanted as if it was owed to him. The world didn't owe Joe a damn thing, he just hadn't figured that out yet.

Poor guy, Logan thought as he pulled the papers the police had given him out of a drawer and looked them over. Joe had once lived in a virtual mansion, now he lived in a crappy apartment in one of the poorer parts of town.

Logan did some internet sleuthing and found out Joe was unemployed, drawing unemployment, and had very little going for him. Obviously, the guy still lived in his glory days. His Facebook was littered with pictures of what Joe considered the good ole days. Many of the pictures had Kiely in them, her eyes two hard flecks of color, harder and colder than icicles.

Those were days when Logan had lived in fear. Not knowing if he'd be assaulted in some way by guys like Joe. Not knowing what fresh torture the pack of assholes at his school would put him through. He'd been a quiet, studious kid who just wanted to get it all over with. He'd been so eager to get out of the area that he'd even taken early college courses to get some of them out of the way.

It was strange, sometimes, being back. He'd remember things as he drove through town, things that had happened or people that were gone now. Some had moved away, leaving empty homes and businesses, while others had died. And not a single person here remembered him.

That was fine with him. It was the way he wanted it.

He'd dealt with bullies from kindergarten until the day he graduated as valedictorian of his high school. He hadn't cared about the honor, however. He just wanted to be gone. He'd gone to his graduation because his parents wanted it, but they hadn't known about the years of abuse he took.

His parents worked hard at two different factories that had since closed down. Back then they often worked double shifts and weekends too, just to make ends meet. At least they'd been smart and only had one child. Logan always thought the pair, who'd conceived him when they were still in high school, would have separated eventually if it hadn't been for him. Having him taught them both a lesson.

When he was very young, they had to hire babysitters on the weekends, but during the week one or other had always been home. They worked different shifts, his mom was on first and his father on second, so he never saw them together. Except for the vacations they dragged him on.

Even those stopped when he got old enough to be home alone while they went away. All he did when he went with them was stay in the room and read, so they started to leave him home to read. At least they could have some alone time then.

The buyer showed up at 3:10 pm, five minutes early, but as he'd demanded in the note, Keily showed the woman right in.

"Hi, Denise, good to see you again." Logan shook the woman's hand and looked her over.

Denise was in her early 30s and of average height, but there wasn't much that was average about her other than that. She had amazing blue eyes, black hair, and a body made for sin. Logan looked her over again and felt…nothing.

What the hell was wrong with him?

"Would you like anything, Denise? We have a variety of drinks we can offer, or can I get something for you at the café across the street?" Keily offered civilly, a bland smile on her face.

"Coffee would be great, Keily. I've been driving all day and my eyes are just so blurry it's ridiculous." Denise smiled at Keily with a grateful sigh and then turned back to Logan. "Hi there, Logan, how are you?"

"I'm great, Denise, have a seat." Keily looked at him while he pointed Denise to the chair in front of his desk.

"I'll have a Coke please, Keily." She hadn't said a word to him, she hadn't since lunchtime, but the mere fact that she was still there told him she wanted to know if he needed anything.

"Of course, Mr. Sinclair," Keily murmured, her head down. She walked out of the door without another word and he frowned.

"You've upset her, I see," Denise said with a magical glitter to her dark blue eyes. Her face was just as lovely as the rest of her, but while Logan could appreciate that she was beautiful, she didn't do anything for him.

"I was a bit abrupt with her earlier. I'll have to apologize at some point." He wouldn't but the buyer didn't need to know that.

They'd known each other since Logan had come back to South Carolina. The company that employed her had offices on this coast too and she'd been the buyer for them from the start. Logan was comfortable with her and they'd built a good rapport together.

The fact that she was married to a woman made it easier to see her as a businesswoman and not a potential conquest. Not that the fact that she was married to a woman made a difference, it was the fact that she was married. He left those women alone.

Dating a married woman was even worse than

dating an employee, in his opinion. Some might disagree, and he knew plenty that did, but his run-in with Joe reminded him why he maintained that opinion. Even though Keily had divorced him, Joe still thought of her as his wife. As his. She was free and if she weren't his employee Logan would have her in his bed in an instant, but she was.

And Joe still thought she was his wife.

She wasn't but the reminder was still there. She'd been married once, and she was his employee. Angry husbands weren't something Logan wanted to deal with. An angry ex-husband that made it his business to punch Logan was a different matter.

Denise brought the conversation back around to the task at hand and Logan focused on that instead of his current problems. Problems plural, when you counted Joe.

Keily would have to testify against her ex, he thought, an hour later when Denise left, happy with the bargain they'd struck. That wouldn't make her very comfortable, but she hadn't said anything about it, other than to apologize to him the day after the event.

He'd ignored the text at the time, too tempted to cancel his flight and go back to her place to finish what he'd started. He'd nearly done that more times than he could count. He'd find himself with his phone in hand, the airline's number ready on the screen. All he had to do was put his thumb on the button, but he'd shut his phone off instead and headed to the airport.

Now she was out there, sad and alone.

He didn't know if she'd made amends with her sister, but he guessed she hadn't. Her eyes lacked any kind of sparkle when she came in this morning, even though she did her job as efficiently as ever and had been dressed appropriately. There was just something missing there. Maybe Joe had come back to her apartment, given her a hard time.

He'd ask her, but…but.

It would just open the door to a personal conversation and he didn't want to do that. He wanted the platonic, business relationship they had. He did.

He didn't, but it's what he'd have to settle for. Keily was off-limits. It was that simple.

"I'm going out." He said to her as he left his office, his suit jacket hooked on a finger and slung over his right shoulder. "I won't be back today."

"Of course, Logan." The same answer she'd given him earlier.

He'd give just about anything to see her smile again, and even more to feel her against his body, so warm and tight and ready for sex. He couldn't have that, he reminded himself as he climbed into his car and drove out to the street. He might have anything money could buy, he might have power now, but Keily Matthews

Miller, former cheerleader and ex-wife of a local foot-ball legend, was still out of reach.

He settled into his leather seat with the heating coils beneath the leather on, and headed out to the nearest highway. He'd drive, he decided, just drive for a while until he felt calm again. Then he'd go back to his own lifeless enormous house and tie himself up in knots about her all over again.

He put on some music and drove until the sunlight dimmed and streetlights started to flicker on. Alone, he stopped at a fast-food restaurant, grabbed some tacos, and then headed home. He opened an imported beer he took out of the fridge and sank down in a black leather recliner. The TV came on with the flick of a button and he set it to play music.

He hated most new television programs and he rarely had time to watch anything, anyway. Music was something he could always listen to, though.

Music had been his escape all those years when he'd come home to a quiet house after a beating or a day of being taunted for not being athletic. The kids at school had called him everything they could think of, and some things he'd never expected, but he'd taken it all quietly, knowing that one day it would all be over and he could live free without their voices.

Except for days like today, when he couldn't escape the memories. The final assault tried to drift into his brain, but it was something he rarely allowed himself to think about. As soon as his mind conjured images of a flickering campfire he stood up and went to stare out of the windows of the darkened house, his tacos and beer forgotten.

He heard cars zoom past on the road not too far away, wondering if they were all eager to get home to their families or partners, ready for some peace and quiet. Those with children likely wouldn't get it, he thought with a pitying smile, but the others might. They might have a night with no memories, while others would drown their sorrows in one addiction or another.

He walked back to his chair, unwrapped the tacos, and ate them despite the fact they were almost cold. A taco was a taco, even bad ones from crappy fast food places.

There was a bar not far from the house and when he was done with his food Logan decided to change his clothes and head out for a drink. Maybe he'd find a willing partner he could bring home and he'd get Keily out of his head for five minutes. He stepped into the bar fifteen minutes later and looked around.

It was the kind of place businessmen like him would come in the evenings to play pool and have a quiet drink, away from their cares and problems. It was dimly lit but music played just a notch too loud. Logan wasn't there for conversation though.

He walked up to the redhead barmaid and ordered a scotch. She brought it to him with a saucy smile and bedroom eyes, but she worked too close to where he lived. Not suitable for a quick roll in the hay. If she was clingy, she'd know where he lived and could walk to his place.

He spotted a woman on her own in the corner, with blonde hair so similar to Keily's that for a second, he thought it was her. The woman turned, as if she felt his eyes on her, a question in her eyes. *What do you want?*

Her eyes were brown but cold and unemotional, so Logan looked away. Suitable, fuckable, but not what he wanted. He waited, watched women and men come and go, but didn't see anyone that raised even a hint of interest.

It took him an hour to figure out what the problem was. He could have any of the women he'd seen if he'd wanted them, but none of them were Keily. Only she would do.

That was a huge problem. He couldn't have her.

He left the bar and walked home. Alone.

18

Logan

The games continued the next day. He wasn't sure why anymore. Keily wasn't anything like she'd been when she first walked in his door, yet he still felt a need to make sure she knew who was boss.

Him.

It was like he had some childish need to make her pay for all the things that had happened to him when he lived in King's Hill as a child. He needed to break her as he'd almost been broken all those years ago. Perhaps it was only that she was an easy target, a convenient target, but he suspected it was something much deeper than that.

He'd wanted to bring her to her knees the first day he saw her in his office. He'd wanted to see her on her knees, quite literally. He'd wanted to crush out that sparkle of confidence that made her gray eyes seem so knowing, and he was almost there.

She'd left his office moments ago, her face flushed with suppressed anger, with her eyes on the verge of something she hadn't decided on yet. Defeat or rage?

Which would win?

Logan didn't know, but he did know that he was enjoying the show. There was a quiet whisper deep in the back of his brain somewhere, a whisper that said he was wrong for treating Keily like a dog, that said he was no better than the bullies he'd lived with in his younger days. But he squashed that whisper just like he squashed the hope in her eyes this morning.

She'd come in with a spring in her step and a smile on her face, despite the way he acted the day before. She had a little bit of vigor in her step again, even though he piled on the criticisms and stopped sending her emails about the things she'd done well at the end of each day. He wondered if leaving yesterday had been a mistake.

He'd needed to get away from the office, from her, but it seemed that time away had given her a break. That wouldn't do.

With a cold glare, he sent her out to the factory to get a form. A form she told him could be emailed to him, but he insisted she go fetch it for him. Her face had turned pink when he insisted and her eyes narrowed, but she didn't reply. She simply turned around and walked out of his office.

She'd be back in a few minutes and Logan took that time to pour some more coffee and settle back into his chair. It was a plush, white leather chair and was one of the most comfortable he'd ever sat in. He swung around in it a little as he waited, not really thinking anything at all for a few minutes.

Other than about how tempting she was when she was mad.

Which was exactly what he shouldn't be thinking about, he reminded himself and stood up. He went to the window and looked out at the town without actually seeing anything. His thoughts were jumbled around again, and he wondered if maybe it was time to call it quits in South Carolina.

He'd never let Keily beat him, not at anything, but he had a feeling this was a battle he couldn't win. If he slept with her, he'd lose. If he fired her, he'd lose again. PAs could be replaced, of course, but Keily was very good at her job. It'd take months to have an assistant as competent as she'd quickly become. She was almost…indispensable.

But so damn annoying, too.

He wasn't sure why she annoyed him so much, she didn't necessarily have any bad habits. The mere fact that she existed seemed to annoy him beyond belief. Or maybe he just didn't want to admit to himself just how attracted he was to her.

Fuck.

"Here you are, Mr. Sinclair."

Back to that again are we, he noted she called him by his last name. Well, fine then.

He took the form she offered in her slim hand and he noted how delicate and pretty her hands were. The kind of hands meant to be admired, that might appear in old-fashioned dish detergent ads. Not the kind that should be typing emails and letters for a dickhead like him.

"This is the wrong form." He said without even taking it from her. "Go back and get the correct form, Keily."

"But this is the E-17, the one you asked for." She sputtered out before she clenched her jaw and looked down at the floor, not at him. She was hiding her anger and that made his spine straighten a little more. With lips thinned so flat they were nearly nonexistent she spoke again. "Which form do you want from the factory, sir?"

The words came out full of venom and Logan suspected she was letting her anger win, not defeat. She still had some fight in her. That meant he could play with her a little longer. Every time she rallied back from depression and expressed her frustration as anger, he knew he could push her a little further. A little harder, and he did that now with a twisted glee he didn't allow to appear on his face.

"I need the 3-CW, Keily. Now, turn around and go back to fetch it like a good girl." He stopped himself from patting her on the head. That might be a step too far.

Plus, being that close to her was dangerous. Even with three feet of empty air between them, he could faintly smell her perfume, something light and citrusy that suited her, made her more appealing. He didn't want her to be appealing and glared at her as irrational anger bloomed in his mind all over again. Why couldn't she go a day without that fucking perfume?

"Yes, Mr. Sinclair." She turned around and left the office again, her coat still on over the black skirt and red sweater she'd worn that morning.

Those heels, he really did love those heels and he'd miss them if she quit.

He answered a call on his cell phone and watched her come back into his office with a warning on her face. A warning he didn't listen to. Fuck her warnings.

She placed the form on his desk, stared down at it for a moment, then turned and left his office. He was about to be a dick and send her back for another one, a totally different form, but she closed his door.

What the hell?

Who did she think was boss here?

"What the fuck, Keily? Why did you close my door?" He asked as he flew out of his chair and to the door.

She turned to him, her face a blank mask, and blinked. Nothing else, she didn't speak, she didn't raise her eyes to his, she just blinked. Once.

Her head tilted slightly after a moment, but she still didn't speak.

Had he pushed her too far?

He had been unbearable lately and he knew he'd nitpicked the stupidest shit, but had he done enough to completely...break her brain? There was nothing behind her eyes, nothing at all.

"Keily?"

She blinked again, her eyes came up to his in question, and some evil little shit deep down in his brain decided now was the time to push just a little bit more.

"You do not close my door unless I tell you to, do you understand me?" His voice was low, carefully controlled, with just enough anger to let her know he wasn't playing. As usual, since that night when her ex-husband punched him. That dickhead.

"Yes, Mr. Sinclair." Her voice was as dead as her eyes, toneless and without the usual sultriness that made up the whole package that was Keily Matthews.

"What the fuck is wrong with you?" Anger bloomed fully in his brain now and he couldn't stop it. That evil little shit that must be his inner child came out full force, intent on making her cry.

He wanted to see her cry. Just once.

The way he used to cry at home when he was alone because both his parents were at work and wouldn't hear him.

Perhaps he needed help, or maybe he just needed someone to talk to besides himself, but he'd never had either. Once he learned that he was on his own in the world he'd kept his thoughts, his problems to himself. Therapy was out of the question too. He didn't see the point in paying someone to tell him what he already knew.

He was fucked in the head, but he could build an empire like he was a god.

"You know Keily, if you were any more useless, you'd be a rock. Strike that, even rocks can serve as decorations in a garden. They can hold back earth banks that are about to cause a landslide. They can be climbed. You though? You can't even get the right form or the right food for me." Never mind that he'd deliberately sent her out with the wrong instructions routinely. "I bet you were all alone for Christmas because your family is too ashamed of you to spend time with you."

A single tear formed in her left eye, but she didn't move. Glee at the power he had over her emotions became a drug, something he didn't know you could be addicted to.

"You've taken advantage of everyone you know, haven't you? Your ex-husband, your sister, your parents. That's why you only have one friend, right? Even though you live in your hometown and should have at least one friend that you've known since kindergarten. You aren't worth knowing. Everyone you know has walked away from you at some point because you just have nothing to give in that dead little heart of yours." He knew it wasn't all true, he'd seen how kind she was to Rosa, he knew the women were close friends, but he suspected he knew why she had nobody else. And he'd just spewed reality out to her.

He told himself someone had to do it as he noticed the stack of mail on her desk. Mail for him that she hadn't sorted yet. It was neatly stacked on her desk, ready for her, but she hadn't sorted it out yet.

"What the hell is that? Is that my mail? Fucking hell, Keily. You can't even manage to bring me my mail on time. If I knew you wouldn't end up homeless, without a car or any prospects, because believe me I won't give you a good reference if you leave here, I'd just fire you." He was rambling now and knew it but there were two more tears, and more forming in her dead eyes. She didn't wipe them away or even change her expression.

She just took his abuse and fuck, he felt like he was on a mad high, one he didn't want to climb down off of.

"If I didn't feel sorry for you, Keily, you'd be gone. It's charity that keeps you here, nothing else. And now that your husband has assaulted me, well, I think I might have run out of charity. I'll let you know by the end of the day whether you're out of a job or not."

He walked away at that point. He paused just as a sob escaped her pretty pink lips, but still her expression didn't change. She was still in there, somewhere, but she was broken. Maybe not completely shattered, but she was definitely broken.

He went to his office, closed the door, and went to sit behind his desk. He knew he could be in deep shit with what he'd just said to her, the way he'd treated her lately, but for the first time in his life, he didn't care about the business, or his empire, the fact that he'd made every person that ever called him a loser a liar. He just wanted to break Keily.

He'd risked it all to break her and those silvery tears that sparkled on her face, wetting her skin as they slid down her cheeks to pool at the corners of her mouth that then produced the most beautiful sound he'd ever heard were worth it all.

Logan hadn't started his day planning to break Keily, but something snapped in him early. Some irrational part of his mind couldn't stand being near her anymore and decided he'd make her wish she'd never stepped foot into the building. His building.

She'd had the audacity to step into his building and ask him for a job. He had a feeling she'd regret that for the rest of her life. And when she came back tomorrow for more? Well, he'd think of some way to make sure she went home the same way she'd go today. Alone and without anyone to turn to. The fact that he wanted her to turn to him was a failing he wouldn't think about right now. Not when he'd just shattered her completely.

19

Keily

*E*nough was enough.

Keily swiped at the tears on her face, stood up from her seat, and grabbed her bag from under the desk. She paused to stare down at the bundle of keys in her hand. Office keys, house keys, the keys to her storage unit at the apartment, her car keys, and the keys to Violet's door that she hadn't returned yet.

Logan was right about one thing; she'd taken advantage of her sister and guilt had eaten at her for a while now about it. She'd make that up to her sister somehow. When she dug her way out of the crater she was about to make of her life.

She didn't care if she lost the apartment, or the car, or the money he paid her. She wasn't taking his abuse anymore. It didn't matter if she couldn't get him off her mind, that she'd taken his dickish behavior for months because of how she felt when she was around him. No amount of desire or awareness, sometimes raw need, was worth taking the abuse he'd just dished out to her.

For a while, she'd turned her brain off, a trick she learned back in her pageant days. Smile vacantly but prettily for long enough and people believed you were alive. Turn your mind off and you totally forgot that people you didn't know were looking at you, hungry to figure out how to exploit you for their own gain.

She continued to use it during her cheerleading years, when she had an injury, or her period arrived with killer cramps. Smile, pretend you aren't hurting, and make people believe the lie you're telling them. She'd almost given in to it completely, but when Logan made that remark about how he'd let her know if she had a job at the end of the day, well, that did it.

That fucking well did it.

With a deep breath, another quick swipe of her face to make sure it was dry, and the keys clutched in her hand, she got up and calmly walked to Logan's door. Normally she wouldn't go near that door if it was closed. It meant he didn't want to be disturbed.

Logan could stick it where the sun didn't shine for all she cared. She was done with him, and if he already planned to give her a bad reference, well fuck, she might as well earn it, right?

He started to yell at her as soon as she opened the door but ducked instead as she launched the keys at his head. "Here, take these, and fuck you, Logan. I quit."

"You what?" He asked softly once he'd sat back up and put the keys on his desk.

"I quit. Take your fucking bullshit about how useless I am and shove it. If you weren't so busy playing games, you'd see I run myself ragged for you. I work all damn day, every day, for you. And what do I get? Childish games and your abuse. Well, I'm done with it, Logan. I'm done with you. You couldn't pay me to stay here with you one more day, so fuck your 'I'll let you know by the end of the day if you still have a job'. I don't give a fuck what you decide, because I'm done." Her voice shook when she started to speak but by the time she'd finished she was steady, strong, ready for whatever he had to dish out.

He stood up and walked over to her, his gaze steely and hard despite the warmth it usually held. She backed up, eager to be out of his office now, but the door was closed. When he finally stopped advancing on her, her back was pressed into the wooden panel and her face was up to his, defiant even as he stared down at her, his nostrils flared.

"You quit?" He asked it softly, his eyes locked to hers and she felt her pulse race. He was so close.

Fuck, he was an absolute dick, but he was so close and he smelled so good, and why the hell couldn't she look away from those stormy, angry eyes?

"Fuck you." She spit it out at him and let the fire of long-suppressed rage flow through her veins. He could go straight to hell, attraction or not.

"Fuck me?" He scoffed with a smirk that made her fury burn hotter.

"Fuck you. Fuck you very much, Logan." She reached for the doorknob, ready to leave, if he'd just stop staring at her with eyes that were suddenly clear of anger and animosity.

"As luck would have it..." He lifted a finger to her face, let it slide down her cheek and along her jaw until the fingertip was directly over her racing pulse. "You can now."

With that last sentence spoken she felt his lips pressed into hers hungrily as he pushed himself into her. Keily's brain felt as if it actually pulsed as she felt every inch of him against her and his tongue swept out to open her lips.

Anger receded into the background as she clutched at his head to hold him to her. Months of denied desire took the place of the need to get away from him and all she wanted, all she needed, was his body next to hers.

It was probably a better idea to walk out, to let him have his little empire of fucked up games, but she couldn't walk away. She'd dreamed of this moment for months and she needed to feel someone human next to her. She needed to feel Logan around her, over her.

Logan pulled away from her long enough to stare down into her eyes and she didn't let him see the uncertainty, the anger she felt towards him, she let him see the desire and nothing more.

"Tell me you want me, Keily." He murmured against her lips, his eyes an inch from hers.

"I want you, Logan." She felt like she was betraying herself, but she could not deny that she wanted him. It was simply the truth.

Logan's body swayed toward her and then away, as if he still hadn't made his mind up about what was going to happen next. But Keily knew, she saw it in his eyes. He was as hungry for her as she was for him.

His lips rocked onto hers and her hands clutched at him, to draw him to her, to stop the swaying so she could once again feel that hard ridge of him pressed into her. Ready for her.

This might be the most idiotic decision of her life, but it was done now. If he wanted her here in his office, he could have her. Neither of them made any promises so even if all she had was this moment, she'd take it and walk away knowing that he hadn't broken her. Not completely. She'd have scars, but she'd live. Big girls always do.

"I'm going to fuck you, Keily," he said, as if she didn't have a say in the matter, but that was fine because she wasn't going to say no anyway. His right hand slid down to her hip to bunch the material of her skirt up in his palm. When he'd exposed the light blue silk panties she wore, he slid his fingers between her skin and the front panel.

A shiver of pleasure raced up her spine as she felt the pressure of his hand against her in an intimate touch she hadn't expected to feel after she'd thrown the keys at him. Her eyes locked on his while his fingers slid further down, to the slick skin hidden deep inside her panties. His lips brushed against hers and she ached to plead with him for more.

"Oh yes, I'm so going to fuck you." His tongue flicked out to lick at her lips just as his fingers found the one spot that she wanted him to touch the most. His finger pressed into that spot, teased it as if he knew exactly how she liked it. The exact way she did it when she was completely alone. "I'm going to have every inch of you before the day is over with."

No promise of anything more than a day of sex, but she'd take it. It was all she wanted. Just a taste of the man that drove her insane with anger and need.

When he dropped to his knees she gasped in

surprise. That was her job, surely? But she didn't protest, couldn't, when he tore the panties away from her body and replaced his finger with this tongue. A very talented tongue, too.

Shaky fingers dug into his hair and she began to move on his mouth. She could kind of remember feeling like this with her vibrator, like she was on the cusp of something incredible, but even when she'd got herself off, she knew that there was more, something she was missing. Logan was about to show her what that missing thing was.

Her calves began to tremble, the steep height of her heels kept her legs at an uncomfortable angle, but she'd seen him looking at the shoes more than once. That's why she wore them often. Now she wanted to rest against his desk but held herself up by sheer will alone. She would not fall to her knees. Not for Logan.

His fingers dug into the silky skin of her outer thighs as if to order her to stand still, but she ignored him. She ignored his orders and moved her hips, moved on his tongue and his lips as he devoured her whole.

"Don't you dare stop, Logan. For once, keep your mouth shut and do what it was made to do." She couldn't believe the words that came out of her mouth, but maybe it was his own fault.

He'd spent months turning her into what he wanted and now he'd have to deal with what he'd created.

Pleasure built within her from that spot he sucked and teased, and she felt something growing within her, that intense thing she'd never been able to capture for herself. She'd got off before, knew what it meant to come, but this was something entirely different. It started in her lower abdomen, it stole her breath as his tongue fed on her and his fingers clutched at her, as she imagined what was coming next.

When he slid a hand between her slick thighs and found her entrance, she gasped again. Anticipation made her catch her breath again, and she took short gasps of air in as he slid into her with two of his long, thick fingers.

In her head she heard him whispering, ordering her to come for him so that's what she did. Only it was so much more than that. For a brief moment that felt like forever, Keily was certain she was about to turn inside out.

Her back arched on the first wave and her nipples turned into hard little points while her mind turned off completely to everything but his tongue and the pleasure it gave her. In his office, against his door, Keily felt real pleasure, the kind that didn't seem to want to end. She was aware of the noises she made and didn't care. All there was in the world now was Logan's tongue and another wave of pure bliss.

When she pushed at his head, the sensations buzzing all the way up to her ears, he pulled away and stood up.

He stared at her, still uncertain until he saw her all but completely clothed but satisfied, for now. "You look so damn fuckable right now."

"Then do it already. You aren't my boss any more. So, fuck me." Keily couldn't see her own eyes but she knew they were full of the dare she wanted him to take. All he had to do was… take her.

"In my office?" He asked as if considering it, but not certain he would agree. She knew it was just a ruse.

"In your office, Logan." She moved to his desk, pushed him gently out of the way, and leaned over. She moved nonchalantly, as if she didn't know the effect, she had on him. "Right here."

She turned her head back to look at him over her shoulder and she saw the way he fought for control. She might not be a seductress in her real life, but she could pretend for a minute or two. She could bring him to his knees again, if she wanted to.

That knowledge filled her with power, the kind he probably didn't want her to have, but fuck him. He'd started this war.

"Keily." He choked off and looked back at the door.

"Lock it." She instructed and he surprised her when he did it. "Now, are you going to fuck me or not?"

"I'll fuck you when I'm good and ready, Keily." He

growled as he came up behind her and pulled her up, away from the desk. With rough fingers, he pulled her chin towards his face, until he could kiss her with a brutal savage need that couldn't be denied any longer.

This was a man on the verge, the verge of what she didn't know, but she was about to find out. She allowed him to savage her mouth with his kiss, enjoyed the rough feel of his five o'clock shadow against her tender lips when he slanted his mouth over hers. She leaned back into him, surrendering for now.

This wasn't going to be an easy day, she knew that, but that was alright. She needed him rough, ready to take her and make her his. Later, she'd have him on his knees again. If they both chose to extend the moment to later.

He stole her thoughts when his hands slid up her stomach to her breasts. He pushed her bra away, too caught up in the moment to take any of her clothes off. When the round globes were bare, he took them in his fingers and teased the nipples until she was certain she was going to fall down, unable to hold herself up.

She was on fire again, ready to turn to him, to demand that he pleasure her again, but he grunted in denial. With his face set in stone, Logan turned her, pushed her skirt back up over her waist, and ran his hand along her ass.

"Nice ass, Keily." He said softly and she took the compliment.

"I'm glad you like it."

"I love it, and I'd come all over it any time." He replied softly as if he was considering that possibility.

"You promised me a fucking, Logan." She reminded him, eager to feel him inside of her now.

"And a fucking you will get, Keily. Don't knock anything off my desk."

"I'm not your PA anymore. Fuck whatever's on your desk." She answered him with a hint of anger in her voice. Just enough to make him grip at her waist and do what she wanted him to do…bend her over his desk.

"Shut up, Keily." He ordered as he stripped quickly and came back to stand behind her, condom on and ready for her.

At least he came prepared.

"Fuck me, Logan." She begged prettily, done with games, ready for the show.

"Yes, ma'am." He answered and grabbed her hips with steady hands. "Hang on."

"Shut up and fuck me."

Instead of answering, Logan thrust into her in one smooth motion, filled her completely until she thought she'd never be that full again. He was thick, long, and so damn hard it was amazing.

She didn't complain about the way he stretched her

until it was almost uncomfortable, she simply took it and waited because she knew she'd adjust to it. At some point. Either way, it felt too good to complain about really, so she let him slide into her over and over again.

"I hate you, Keily. I don't know why I'm fucking you." He groaned behind her.

With a smile, she clung to the desk just as her body began to spasm all over again. All over him. She had him, finally, and she might not know how any of this ended, but for now, she was going to take this ride with him and see where it took her. Just before she blew apart one last time, just before a groan stole her voice away, she whispered five little words to him. "I hate you too, Logan."

He followed her to the land where only pleasure existed, voiceless, satisfied, and quiet, at last. In a minute, she'd catch her breath, in a minute she'd decide whether he was worth doing it all over again for. In a minute, she'd decide whether to walk away from him and never look back. For now, she took the pleasure he gave her with greedy need and thrived on it. He thought he'd broken her. Too bad for him he was wrong.

TWISTED INTENTION
~ A billionaire revenge romance series ~
Twisted Beauty
Twisted Love
Twisted Fate

Mafia's Obsession
~ A hot mafia romance series ~
Mafia's Dirty Secret
Mafia's Fake Bride
Mafia's Final Play

Screaming Demons
~ An MC romance series full of suspense ~
Rough Start
Rough Ride
Rough Choice
Rough Patch
Rough Return
Rough Road
Rough Trip
Rough Night
Rough Love

Standalone Contemporary Romance
Billionaire in Vegas
Billionaire Hunt

Billionaire's Game
Billionaire Retreat
Billionaire On Air
A Chance To Love
Somebody To Love
Not Mine To Love

Check out Summer's entire collection at
www.summercooper.com/books

ABOUT SUMMER COOPER

Thank you so much for reading. Without you, it wouldn't be possible for me to be a full-time author. I hope you enjoy reading my books as much as I do writing them.

Besides (obviously!) reading and writing, I also love cuddling my dogs, shouting at Alexa, being upside down (aka Yoga) and driving my family cray-cray!

Get in touch at
hello@summercooper.com
www.summercooper.com

facebook.com/summercooperauthor
instagram.com/summercooperauthor
goodreads.com/summercooper
bookbub.com/profile/summer-cooper

www.ingramcontent.com/pod-product-compliance
Lightning Source LLC
Chambersburg PA
CBHW031232210726
48287CB00003B/755